A SECOND HELPING OF CRAZY

OF CRAZY

COLLECTED STORIES

Titles by John D. Ottini

People Behaving Badly: A Collection of Short Mystery Stories (2015)

A Very Furry Christmas: Holiday Cat Tales (2015)

The Black & Blue Butterfly Tattoo (2017)

The Twisted Road Ahead: An Anthology of Short Stories (2018)

A Fool for Love & Money (2019)

Elevated Madness and Other Stories (2020)

Desperation Kills (2021)

A SECOND HELPING OF CRAZY

OF CRAZY

COLLECTED STORIES

John D. Ottini

Copyright

A Second Helping of Crazy: Collected Stories
© 2022 John D. Ottini
Cover Art by Lou Harper Copyright 2022

ISBN–13: 9798442814958

Dedication

To my parents
for giving me the love and freedom to be the person I've become.

To my wife Nancy
for her continued love, friendship, and support.

To my cat Bella
for bringing a smile to my face every time she greets me at the
front door.

Preface

In ***A Second Helping of Crazy***, I've collected thirteen of my most memorable stories in one volume. Three stories were previously chosen as Finalist in the annual Royal Palm Literary Awards competition, and the rest are a selection of my personal favorites.

I sincerely hope you enjoy reading (or rereading) these stories, as much as I enjoyed writing them.

The stories in this book were previously released in the following publications.

"No Return Address", "Remorse" and "Life Among the Fireflies" were originally published in *Elevated Madness and Other Stories, 2020.*

"Elevated Madness" was originally published in *Writers @ Work – Collection 11 (Florida Writers Association),* 2019.

"One Shot to the Head", "Words to A Kill", "Tormented Heart", Things We Can't Contro1" and "Blame it on the Weather" were originally published in *The Twisted Road Ahead: An Anthology of Short Stories, 2018.*

"Killer Karma", "Hell to Pay", "The Butcher" and "True Confession" were originally published in, *People Behaving Badly: A Collection of Short Mystery Stories, 2015.*

JDO – June 2022

CONTENTS

A Second Helping of Crazy: Collected Stories

A SECOND HELPING OF CRAZY
COLLECTED STORIES

"What sane person could live in this world and not be crazy?"

Ursula K. Le Guin – American Author
(1929-2018)

One Shot to the Head

2018 Finalist in the Royal Palm Literary Awards Competition
(Short Story Genre)

Tyler reached across the table, placed his hand over mine, looked into my eyes and said, "Brie, you look absolutely radiant tonight. Do you have any idea how much I love you?"

I could see my reflection in his dark, sexy eyes, and the sincere look on his face made me want to reach across the table and give him a deep passionate kiss. Instead, I took his hand, kissed it softly and held it to my cheek.

"I love you too, Tyler Mason. You really are the best thing that ever happened to me."

Tyler glanced around the crowded restaurant, leaned forward and whispered, "I know," and burst out in laughter.

I slapped his hand away. "Why do you have to be an ass at such a romantic moment?"

"Oh, come on, Brie. You know I'm kidding. We've been together for five years; you know how I feel about you."

I stretched my left hand across the table, wiggled my fingers and mockingly sang the lyrics from that really bad Beyoncé tune, "If you liked it, then you should have put a ring on it."

Tyler rolled his eyes and was about to reply when the waiter arrived with the check.

"Mademoiselle et Monsieur, I 'ope that the food and service was to your liking?" he said in a heavy French accent.

"You've been wonderful, Marcel. Thank you for making this a memorable evening." Tyler replied.

"Is there anyzing else I can get you or ze young lady?"

"No, I think we are done," replied Tyler, placing his hand over the receipt.

The waiter bowed. "Bien."

"Mercy beaucoup, Marcel," Tyler said, using the only two words of French he knew, and reached inside the front of his blazer.

"I had a wonderful time, Babe," I said. "Thank you for taking me to this fancy place."

"Nothing's too good for my girl," he replied, in a poor imitation of Humphrey Bogart. He reached down to pat his back pockets and gave me a bewildered look.

"Is everything okay?" I asked.

"Yeah, it's fine. I just need to run out to the car for a minute. I'll be right back."

"You don't look fine."

"I think I left my wallet in the glove compartment. I'll be right back," he said, pushed his chair away from the table, got up and walked briskly toward the exit.

When Tyler had told me two weeks earlier that he had something special planned for Valentine's Day, I had no idea he was taking me to Chez Charles for dinner. The evening had been wonderful so far, but I couldn't help but feel disappointed that there was no marriage proposal. I had convinced myself that tonight would be the night, but now I was left wondering if Tyler would ever propose.

During the last five years of us living together, the subject had come up in numerous conversations and Tyler's response had always been, "What's the big rush? When the time is right, we'll get married. Nothing is going to change. I ain't going anywhere, Babe."

Even our parents had been wondering and hinting about a marriage proposal, but Tyler hadn't budged. I knew that he loved me, but the older we got and the more I thought about our relationship, the more I wanted to take the next step and make it legal.

I want a house, a husband, and a family. This living together thing is not enough. Maybe it's time we sit down and have a heart-to-heart conversation, I thought.

I was so deep in thought that I hadn't notice Tyler's return.

He sat in the chair across from me with a peculiar look on his face.

"I did something really stupid, Brie."

"Don't tell me you lost your wallet?" I asked with a panicked tone in my voice.

"No, I didn't lose it, but I'm pretty sure I left it on my end table back at the apartment."

"Are you kidding?"

"Do I look like I'm kidding?"

"This is so embarrassing," I said as I picked up the dinner receipt. "Oh my God, we owe them $235.10. What are we going to do?"

"Do you have any money?"

"Probably thirty-five bucks."

"Shit! What about a credit card?"

"I told you last week, my account was compromised, and the bank is sending me a new card!"

I thought I saw beads of sweat on his forehead. "Shit. I completely forgot."

"What are we going to do?"

"Don't panic. I have a plan."

"This had better be good, Tyler. I was hoping you'd ask me to marry you tonight! I had no idea the evening would involve washing dishes instead—or even worse, going to jail," I said as moisture welled up in the corners of my eyes.

"Calm down, Babe. No one is going to jail, or washing dishes," he replied with a nervous laugh.

"Sorry, but you don't look or sound very convincing."

He glanced around the room, then back at me. "Here's what I want you to do. Order another glass of wine or a cup of coffee. That should buy me enough time to go home and get my wallet."

"But Marcel already gave us the check."

"So what? Tell him we changed our minds. It happens all the time. It shouldn't take more than twenty minutes tops. You can stall for that long, can't you?"

"Do I have a choice?" I asked in a snarky tone. "What if he asks me where you are?"

"Make something up." He kissed my cheek and walked away.

I looked down at my napkin, desperately hoping that our waiter would not come around for the next twenty minutes.

Unfortunately, when I raised my eyes I noticed Marcel coming towards me.

"Is zere a problem, Mademoiselle?" He stared at Tyler's empty chair.

"Not at all, Marcel. My boyfriend received a telephone call of a private nature," I said, lowering my voice, "and had to step outside for a moment. He'll be right back."

"Ah, I see. Can I get Mademoiselle somezing while she is waiting?"

"Yes. I would love another glass of the Chateau Giscours Bordeaux."

"As you wish," he replied, grabbing the check from the table.

I knew it wasn't true, but at that moment it felt like everyone in the restaurant was staring at me.

I couldn't remember the last time I felt so embarrassed. No, on second thought, I did remember. It was on my high school trip to Europe. We were travelling through Spain when our tour bus stopped so we could use the public restrooms. I had the misfortune of walking out of the lavatory with the toilet paper I had used to cover the seat hanging from the waistline of my jeans. I'll never forget the look on my classmates' faces and the laughter as my best friend Laura desperately tried to remove the paper hanging from my jeans before anyone else saw it.

Just the thought of that incident made me want to crawl under the table and hide. And now I felt the same way.

Marcel returned with a glass of Bordeaux. I sat for the next fifteen minutes sipping the wine as slowly as possible and glancing at my watch.

My cell phone rang twice before I managed to retrieve it from my purse. I didn't recognize the number, but a voice in my head told me to answer it anyway.

"Hello?"

"Brie! It's me."

"Tyler? I almost didn't pick up the call. Whose phone are you using? I don't recognize the number. Why didn't you use your cell phone?"

"The battery is dead."

"Seriously?" I said, my voice going high-pitched. Tyler began to say something, but I interrupted him. "Are you on your way? I don't think I can stall much longer."

"Sorry, Sweetheart, but we have a problem."

My throat went dry, but I managed to ask, "What do you mean 'we' have a problem?"

"I was in such a hurry to get home as quickly as possible that I got pulled over for speeding."

"What? Why would you do something so careless?"

"Careless! Do you have any idea what it felt like having to leave you at the table like I did? The look on your face broke my heart. I knew that I had to get back to you as quickly as possible."

"What are you saying? Are you implying that this mess is my fault?" I said, my voice getting louder than I wanted it to.

Now everyone in the restaurant was indeed staring at me.

Tyler was quick to apologize. "Well, of course not! That's not what I meant. I felt bad about forgetting my wallet and leaving you there alone. I should have been more careful driving and I definitely regret running the red light."

"You ran a red light?!"

"I made a poor decision. What can I say?"

"Where are you?"

"I'm sure that someday we'll look back on this whole mess and laugh about it."

"Quit stalling and tell me. Where the hell are you and when will you get here?"

"I don't know."

"You don't know where you are?"

"No, I don't know when I'll get there."

"I'm freaking out here, Tyler. That's not the answer I need to hear."

"I know, but I have no idea how long it will take to sort this mess out."

"Sort out what?" I asked, bewildered. "What is it you aren't telling me?"

Tyler replied in such a faint voice that I didn't hear him the first time, but the second time was loud and clear. "I'm at the police station on Broadway."

A swear word sat on the tip of my tongue, but I glanced at the tables around me and refrained from using it.

"You're at the station because you received a traffic violation? I don't get it!"

"Well, that and the fact that I didn't have my license or any form of identification."

"Tell them you'll go home, get your ID and return with the information they need."

I heard Tyler take a long breath before responding. "Wish it were that simple. I was very upset when the cop pulled me over and I tried to explain the situation, but he couldn't care less. He just kept repeating 'license and registration' and then I said something that in hindsight I shouldn't have said."

"So, he took you in to the station!"

"Yes."

I could feel myself losing control. "Oh my God, oh my God…"

"Calm down, Brie. Everything will be okay. It's just a show of power, they're going to release me with a minor infraction charge."

"It's not okay! What am I supposed to do about the restaurant bill?"

"I'm at the police station and you're worried about a stupid dinner check? Are you kidding me?"

We both went silent for a moment, each of us trying not to say anything that we'd regret later.

Tyler finally broke the silence. "I'm sure that if you explain the situation to the manager, he or she will understand. I've seen you turn on the charm when you need to."

"I can't believe you did this to me. You owe me big time."

"I'm really sorry, Brie, I never meant for this to happen. If I could reset the day, you know I would. I love you, Babe. You're the best thing that ever happened to me too."

"Arrgh! How can I stay mad at you if you won't shut up?"

"Just talk to the restaurant manager, I'm sure this isn't the first time something like this has happened."

"That's what I'm afraid of."

"I gotta go, Brie. They're calling my name. I'll pick you up as soon as I can. I'll call you from the apartment. If worse comes to worst, call Rick, maybe he can front you the money or at the very least give you a ride home."

"Fine, I'll see you later."

"Love you."

"I love you too, but at this moment I can't think of a reason why."

Tyler hung up the phone and I signaled Marcel to the table. I decided that I'd rather take my chances with the manager than borrow money from our neighbor Rick and have to explain this embarrassing situation.

Marcel arrived at the table sporting an inquisitive look on his face. "Is somezing wrong, Mademoiselle?"

"Yes. Can I please speak to the manager?"

"Is it somezing I did?" he asked, pointing at himself in a defensive manner.

"Not at all, Marcel. You've been wonderful. This has nothing to do with the food or the service."

Marcel smiled in relief and said, "As you wish, Mademoiselle."

He left me sitting in panic mode, wondering what I was going to say to the manager. A part of me hoped the manager was male, so I might have a better chance at turning on my feminine charm.

You can do this, Brie, I kept telling myself as I waited for the manager to arrive.

As luck would have it, the manager was indeed male, but as he approached the table I noticed that he had a striking resemblance to a very pissed off Robert DeNiro in *Goodfellas*.

"Hello, my name is William Ragusa," he said, extending his hand. "I'm the manager. I understand you'd like to speak with me."

I shook his hand. "Very nice to meet you, Mr. Ragusa. My name is Brie LaSalle and I wonder if I could speak to you privately."

"Does this have something to do with your server?" he asked, staring at Marcel.

"No. Marcel has been wonderful."

"Is there an error on the bill?"

"No," I said, swinging my head side to side like an idiot.

"Then what is it?"

"I would rather not discuss this in the middle of this crowded restaurant."

"I understand. Please follow me back to my office. Marcel, I'm going to need your assistance."

"I told you that Marcel has nothing to do with this."

"I heard you, Mademoiselle, but for legal reasons I can't take you back into my office without a witness being present. I hope you understand?"

"Sure," I replied, thinking, *can this possibly get more embarrassing than it already is?*

I followed the manager and Marcel through the busy kitchen to an unexpectedly large room at the rear of the building.

The office was sparingly decorated with just four pieces of furniture—an oversized desk, leather chair and two comfortable high-backed chairs for visitors. The walls were adorned with paintings of the Eiffel Tower, the Arc de Triomphe, Notre Dame and the Louvre. Behind the desk was a bookshelf with framed restaurant reviews from the local newspapers and magazines and prominent food critics. A diploma in Hospitality Management from Penn State sat in the center of the shelf.

Mr. Ragusa adjusted the photograph of what I assumed was his family on his desk and pointed towards one of the chairs. "Please have a seat, Mrs.—or is it Miss LaSalle?"

"Thank you, and it's Miss."

"So, what can I do for you?"

I nervously ran my fingers through my shoulder-length hair while searching for the right words to begin the conversation.

"Come, Miss LaSalle. Whatever the problem is, it can't be that bad."

"It's not so much bad as it is embarrassing. The long and short of it is that I can't pay my dinner bill."

Mr. Ragusa looked at Marcel and smiled. "I'm sure you have a good explanation as to how this happened?"

"Of course, I do."

"Is this something that you and your friend do on a regular basis?"

"Absolutely not!" I snapped, then tried to calm down – I wanted to keep him happy.

"Then how did this happen? Please explain."

I took at least five minutes to explain what had happened and, then that long again for groveling and apologizing. The manager gave me a stony-faced expression, so I shut my mouth and waited for his response.

What Mr. Ragusa did next surprised me. He leaned back in his chair and burst out in a frightening laugh.

"Do you seriously expect me to believe that story? Do you have any idea how many times one of my customers has told me one of these crazy stories?"

"It may be a crazy story, but it's the truth, I swear."

Mr. Ragusa leaned over the desk. "So, if you were me, what would you do?"

I felt like he was mocking my every word and I began to feel tears building in the corners of my eyes.

"I'd… I'd expect you to believe me and to give me the benefit of the doubt."

The manager looked at Marcel, who hadn't made a sound since we entered the office. "Do you believe her, Marcel?"

Marcel shrugged his shoulders. "She seems like a nice lady... I sink maybe she is telling ze truth."

Mr. Ragusa nodded his head and said, "I believe her too."

At that moment all I wanted to do was to get the hell out of that office and wring Tyler's neck.

"Thank you so much," I said, breathing a sigh of relief. "I promise I'll be back first thing in the morning to pay the bill. I can assure you that this will never happen again."

"I believe you, Miss LaSalle. Unfortunately, I cannot allow you to leave before you answer one last question."

"What question?"

Mr. Ragusa smiled. "Turn around."

I spun around, half expecting to see the police standing behind me, but instead I saw my mom and dad, Mr. and Mrs. Mason, and Tyler down on one knee holding the largest diamond ring I'd ever seen.

Tyler had a big stupid smile on his face.

"Brie Elizabeth LaSalle. Will you marry me?"

My initial shock turned into tears as I realized what was happening. I stepped toward Tyler, placed one finger under his chin and said, "Yes, I'll marry you, Sweetheart, but first..."

With a thump, my right fist connected with Tyler's left eye and I watched as his head snapped backwards and the ring flew into the air.

* * *

"It took several weeks for his shiner to disappear; we married later that year and have lived happily ever after. Today is our tenth anniversary."

News Channel Two's human interest reporter Chad Black laughs. "Wow, that's one heck of a story. What would you say to the viewers out there who might find this whole story a bit difficult to believe?"

Tyler glances at me, looks around at our party guests and then stares directly into the camera.

"Anyone who chooses not to believe her story does so at their own peril. Right, Honey?"

"You know it, Sweetheart." I make a fist, blow on the knuckles, and punch it toward the camera lens.

The entire room bursts out in laughter.

The camera pans back to reporter Chad Black.

"There you have it folks, the most unusual proposal story you're ever likely to hear. Congratulations, Mr. and Mrs. Mason, on your tenth anniversary. Now back to Bill Barlow in the studio."

Killer Karma

Business at Billy's Tap Room is slow for a mid-Saturday afternoon, but Ace Miller is too preoccupied with customers seated around the bar to give it much thought.

Ace the bartender listens intently as Mrs. Marsalina complains about the latest exploits of her 19-year-old daughter Bella. If they handed out awards for poor judgment, Bella would probably be a finalist in most categories, thinks Ace. The girl's a high school dropout who's been arrested twice for drug possession and now she's had the misfortune of getting impregnated by a man twice her age.

Ace frowns and says, "I feel for you, Mrs. M. If she were my daughter, I'm not sure what I would do."

Mrs. Marsalina shakes her head and takes another sip of Jack Daniels.

Ace is a good listener; at least that's what his customers tell him. The secret to being a good bartender is to listen, sympathize and keep the drinks flowing. Never offer advice unless asked to do so and never argue with a customer. Most folks are like Mrs. Marsalina: they want someone to listen to their sad tale but have no interest in hearing any solution you may wish to offer.

As he wipes off the countertop, he grins and thinks about Mrs. M's plight in life. *Perhaps if she spent less time in bars and more time with her daughter, the results might have turned out differently.*

Mrs. Marsalina isn't exactly a role model for healthy relationships. Married at eighteen, pregnant at twenty, widowed at thirty-five, and in and out of more bad relationships then he cares to remember hearing about. She's not a bad looking woman, but like her daughter she doesn't seem to have much in the way of ambition. She would much rather complain about how her irresponsible daughter is driving her to drinking than actually do something to rectify the situation.

Ace hears the familiar sound of tapping coming from the far end of the counter. He pretends to ignore it and continues listening to Mrs. M's story, but he knows that the tapping will continue until Summerfield gets what he wants, and what he wants is another drink.

With a loud clearing of his throat, Ben Summerfield taps the bottom of his beer mug harder against the bar counter, registering his displeasure at being ignored.

"What the hell does a man have to do to get a goddamn drink around here?"

Ace grins at Mrs. Marsalina, excuses himself and pours another mug of Guinness draft beer. He steps to the far end of the counter and places the glass in front of Mr. Summerfield.

"Here you go, Professor."

"Well, it's about bloody time," Summerfield replies sarcastically.

Ace leans on the counter and says, "Listen, mate. It's not like you're the only customer in the joint who needs a drink. You'd think that after all of them years of teaching that you'd have learned a thing or two about patience."

Summerfield sips a mouthful of beer, pulls out a fresh pack of cigarettes and taps them on the counter. Everyone knows it's against the law to smoke in public establishments, but the regulars at Billy's know that the rule doesn't apply in the Tap Room. Ace hasn't figured out how owner Vladimir gets away with it, but he got the folks at the Board of Health to look the other way. If Ace were a betting man, he'd wager that Vlad has some friends in high places who enjoy free drinks and the occasional fed note with Ben Franklin's picture on it.

Ace doesn't mind his clientele smoking in the bar. If there's one thing that years of bartending have taught him, it's that smokers are also excellent tippers.

Summerfield pulls out a cigarette, lights it and takes a deep drag before speaking.

"Please don't lecture me on patience and you know that I hate it when you call me Professor. I'm no longer a professor and haven't been for years. That was another life."

"Sure thing, Professor," replies Ace, smiling. "I'll stop calling you Professor when you stop tapping on the bar every time you need another drink. Do we have a deal?"

Summerfield blows smoke out of his nose and says, "No deal. It's my right as a paying customer to tap on this bar if I feel I'm being ignored by my bartender."

Ace laughs, shrugs his shoulders, and says, "Whatever you want, Professor," then steps away to attend to other customers.

For more than 20 years, Ben Summerfield was a highly respected science professor. He received accolades from both his students and his colleagues and was twice nominated for 'Teacher of the Year'. The man was somewhat of a celebrity in these parts and would have retired as a respected pillar of the community had it not been for the accident.

Five years ago, his wife Mary was killed in a hit and run incident. She was rear-ended by a driver who drove away from the scene and wasn't arrested until two days later. The driver was the son of a wealthy investment broker who waited until his son sobered up (at least that's what Summerfield suspects) before turning him in to law enforcement.

Mary died from head injuries three days after the accident. The young man who killed her was represented by a slew of high-priced attorneys who managed to get the boy off with minimal jail time and some community service. The prosecutor did his best, but with no witnesses, it was impossible to prove that the boy was drunk at the time of the accident. He was charged with leaving the scene and with reckless driving. The penalty should have been stiffer, but Summerfield suspects the old man's political and law enforcement connections had something to do with the light sentence handed down by the court.

Summerfield filed a civil suit, which was promptly settled out of court. He received a large sum of money in the settlement, but it could never replace his beloved Mary. Devastated and depressed, he decided to take a two-month sabbatical from teaching to heal the pain and bitterness of his loss.

He'd known Mary his entire life. They grew up next door to each other and were sweethearts all through high school. It was a shock when Mary discovered she was pregnant during their first year of college, but Summerfield did the right thing and asked her to marry him. Their parents were not crazy about the situation, but what could they do but be supportive and try to assist the young couple in preparing for a new child?

Ben and Mary agreed that Mary would postpone her education to stay home with the baby while he continued to study for his teaching degree. Mary fully intended to continue her education once the child (a boy) was old enough to begin school, but two years later a daughter arrived, and the plan was put on hold indefinitely.

By the time Summerfield landed his first teaching job, his children Sam and Becky were six and four years of age. Today the kids are grown up and in their twenties. Becky is married to an engineer and pursuing a science degree at California Tech, while Sam is an auto mechanic at a local repair shop.

Once the children were off to college, Mary decided it was finally time to complete her education. She was on her way home from class when the fatal accident happened.

After his sabbatical Summerfield returned to teaching, but it wasn't the same without Mary at his side. His goals and dreams for the future meant little without her and even his students began to notice that Professor Summerfield's heart was no longer in the classroom. He'd show up every day and go through the motions but couldn't wait to go home and numb his pain with alcohol. To his credit, he never gave the appearance of being drunk in class, or so it seemed to his students and colleagues.

For a while he was incredibly good at deception; he even managed to fool himself into believing everything was under control. Even after his terrible accident he is still in denial.

Once again, the tap, tap, tapping can be heard throughout the barroom. Owner Vlad Kucheroff, who has just entered his establishment, looks over at Ace and motions his head towards Summerfield as if to say, *Give the man a drink and shut him up.* Ace acknowledges and responds quickly with another mug of Guinness.

"Listen, mate, you really gotta stop doing that. It's annoying the boss and I don't think you want to get on his bad side."

"Do you mean Vlad the Russian mobster?"

Ace leans in close and whispers, "I suggest you keep your voice down, Professor, unless you want Vlad to have you thrown out on your ass." Ace can see that Summerfield is getting drunk (as he does most days) and doesn't want the poor bastard to make things worse than they already are.

"I'm not afraid of that Russian asshole."

Ace interrupts him and says, "You're drunk, Professor. Please watch what you say about the owner, or I'll stop serving you."

Summerfield opens his mouth to say more but stops when he realizes that Ace means what he says.

"Okay, okay, I'll shut up, but I'm not drunk. You're just as bad as the goddamn cops."

Here we go again, thinks Ace. *The 'woe is me' tale is about to be re-told.* Ace has heard it fifty times and is still amazed at the Professor's delusional insistence that he was wronged by the police.

"The damn liars said I was drunk and out of control, but I wasn't then and I'm not now."

Ace leans his elbow on the counter and says, "I believe they told you that you'd been driving with a blood alcohol level of .14. That's .6 above the legal limit. How can you possibly insist that you weren't drunk?"

Ace realizes that he is breaking one of his bartending rules, to never argue with a customer, but this guy needs a dose of reality if he's ever going to rejoin society as a productive citizen.

"I don't know anything about that, but I'm certain I wasn't drunk. I know better than to drink and drive, and if I got behind that wheel it was because I was in control, not drunk. No one believes me when I say I was framed."

"If you weren't drunk, then how did you lose control of your car and hit that boy on the sidewalk? What reason would the police have to frame you? It doesn't make sense."

Summerfield's face turns red as he points his index finger at Ace.

"That's a bold-faced lie, mister. I never hit him on the sidewalk. The kid ran out into the road. When I realized what was happening, I slammed on the brakes, but it was too late to avoid hitting him. My car slid off the road and onto the sidewalk with the boy pinned underneath it. There was nothing I could do to avoid it," he says, motioning with his hands.

"Right," replies Ace in disbelief, "and every witness who came forward must have been lying when they testified that they saw you lose control of your car, run up on that sidewalk and hit the boy."

Summerfield sighs and confirms, "I never denied hitting the boy, but it wasn't on the damn sidewalk. The little brat ran into the road. As for the witnesses, there were no witnesses," he says defiantly. "Those people who said they witnessed the whole thing are liars."

"Professor, I'm always astonished when you tell your side of the story, not because you believe that your version is true but because I hear no remorse in your voice, and I don't see any on your face."

"Remorse," he says as spit flies from his mouth. "Remorse for what?"

Ace throws his hands up in frustration as Summerfield continues to speak.

"The police and the legal system ruined my career and my life. Why should I feel sorry for that kid? I served three years in jail, lost my job, my license, and a shitload of money in the civil suit. What about me?" Summerfield says loudly. "No one gives a shit about me!"

"Calm down, Professor!"

Summerfield looks around the room, notices the faces staring at him and quietly says, "If that boy had had some parental guidance, he would not have been trying to run across a busy street when the crosswalk was only fifty feet away."

"Oh, man, you're one to talk about parental guidance," replies Ace, flabbergasted.

"What the hell do you mean by that?"

"Never mind. Have another drink and pretend I didn't say anything."

"No, I want to know what you mean by that comment."

"Nothing, Professor," Ace says as he walks away. "It's not worth pursuing."

It's common knowledge that many of the bartenders around town know each other and exchange information about customers who cause problems at their establishments. The bartender at Bennie's Brew House told Ace to watch out for Summerfield's son Sam, who's apparently a chip off the old block, but with a nasty streak. The boy's a hard-drinking regular at a number of local watering holes and is often tossed out for using foul language and inciting disturbances with other customers.

Ace looks over at Summerfield and notices the Professor's head lying on the counter, eyes closed. The bar is pretty quiet at the moment, so he decides to let the old man sleep a bit and maybe sober up before getting him a cab home. He feels sorry for the old fart, knowing that the last few years have been difficult on him, but it's hard to forget what the man did and his lack of remorse over taking an innocent life.

Time goes by and Ace keeps an eye on the sleeping Professor slumped in the corner. Around nine o'clock, business begins to pick up at Billy's and Summerfield is awakened by the sound of laughter and loud voices. He wipes spittle from the side of his mouth, lights up a cigarette and taps his mug on the bar.

Ace looks over and says, "Back from the dead, are we?"

Summerfield grumbles and taps his mug even harder.

"A couple more and I'll be calling you a cab. Do we understand each other?"

"I don't need a cab. I can walk home on my own two feet," Summerfield says defiantly.

"Suit yourself, Professor, but you look a bit unstable to me."

"Unstable? Of course, you would think that!"

"I didn't mean it that way. Don't put words in my mouth. I just want to make sure you get home safely."

Summerfield coughs, rubs his bloodshot eyes, and lights another smoke. He stares off into space and for a moment it looks like he's going to cry. The sadness in his eyes is so overwhelming that Ace is forced to look away.

"You have no idea what I've been through," Summerfield says to no one. "I had a fantastic job, a wonderful wife, two beautiful children and a life that anyone would envy, and it was all taken away in one moment of carelessness."

Ace isn't sure if he means the death of his wife or the death of the child, but he guesses it really doesn't matter; both acts contributed equally to Summerfield's life of misery.

Tears form in Summerfield's eyes, but he speaks no further. He sits quietly drinking his beer and smoking the last of his cigarettes. At eleven o'clock he pays his tab, leaves a tip, stands up and staggers towards the door.

Halfway across the room, he stops, turns towards Ace and says, "I'll see you tomorrow, Ace. Thanks for serving me and for listening to the words of a tired old man."

Ace gives the man a sad smile and says, "Anytime, Profess... I mean Mr. Summerfield. Please be careful walking home. Are you sure I can't call you a cab?"

"No, thanks, young man. It's not a long walk and the cold air will do me good."

Ace gives him a thumbs up and the old man is gone.

On the way home, under the privacy of darkness, Summerfield walks with tears in his eyes. The thought of going back to his dingy little apartment above the grocery store, without anyone to speak to or any reason to wake up in the morning, is breaking his will. He had a falling out with his son Sam, who no longer calls or visits, and his daughter Rebecca is attending college out of state. Thank goodness she's always been an A student and managed to earn several scholarships to pay for college, otherwise who knows what would have happened. There was certainly no way that he could have afforded to pay for her education, especially after he lost everything in the civil lawsuit brought by the dead boy's parents.

How did my life come to this? he thinks, all the while knowing the answer.

"Thank God Mary can't see me this way," he says as his voice cracks with emotion.

Overcome by dizziness, he stops to rest on a bus stop bench. The frigid wind blows flakes of snow into his face, but none of that matters at this moment. As he labors to breathe in and out, he feels a sudden calmness and resolve engulf his body. A feeling he thought he'd lost a long time ago fills him with inner peace and a clarity that's been missing since the death of his wife.

"Mary, I've been such a damn fool. All these years of drowning my sorrow in alcohol. I should have known that the evil drink that led to your death and the death of that poor young man, could never be the solution to my problems."

A man walking by hears Summerfield talking to himself, stops and hands him a ten-dollar bill.

"Get yourself a hot meal, buddy. Life begins anew every morning. God bless you."

He responds by saying, "Thank you, sir, and God bless you too." Summerfield thinks, *if a perfect stranger can believe in me, how can I give up on myself so easily?*

Looking to the night sky, he says out loud, "Tomorrow's a new day, Mary, and I can't go on like this, I just can't. No more alcohol, no more cigarettes. It's time I get a job and get back on my feet. As hard as it may be, this has to stop now."

With newfound pride in his step, he rises from the bench with difficulty and continues his walk home. A familiar tune is playing in his head, one his wife would sing to their babies. The joyful music in his head is enough to distract him from noticing the swirling lights and the screeching sound of car brakes squealing on the road behind him. It isn't until he feels the sharp pain in his side that he realizes what is happening. The out-of-control vehicle hits him, his body becomes airborne and lands against a utility pole where he is pinned by the front bumper. His head rests against the warm hood of the engine, but he can't feel anything below his waist. The iron-rich taste of blood fills his mouth as he struggles to lift his head and open his eyes.

As he begins to lose consciousness, he sees the blurred silhouette of a man walking towards him and a voice speaking words he can barely make out.

"Are you okay, mister? Can you hear me? Are you okay, mister?"

He feels a warm hand touching his face as he takes his final breath, never hearing the words, "Dad! Oh my God, is that you, Dad?"

Life among the Fireflies

I watch as the sun crests the horizon above the corn field. It's late August and I can feel the cold morning breeze that crosses the front porch of our farmhouse. It's six in the morning but I've never felt more awake and ready to face another day. I close my eyes and listen to the chickens clucking in the yard, the horses restless in the corral and the cows mooing in the field.

My morning bliss is interrupted by the sound of my wife's voice.

"Abe? Abraham, can you hear me?"

"Yes, dear, I'm out on the porch."

"Be a dear and lend me a hand with the screen door."

"Sure, sweetheart, I'll be right there," I answer as I push myself up from the rocking chair.

I open the screen door and Dell walks out with two steaming cups of coffee. We sit down on the rockers next to each other.

"It feels like rain," I say as I take a sip of my coffee.

"Yup. That's what the fellow on the TV said this morning."

"Good coffee, Dell!"

"Same old stuff we always drink." She shrugs her shoulders.

"I know, but for some reason it tastes really good this morning."

"Does this have something to do with Joshua leaving today?"

"Course not, I love my grandson. I hate to see him go, but under the circumstances I'm a bit relieved that he's going. We sure don't need him mixed up in this mess."

She puts her cup down on the table next to the rocker. "Speaking of mess, the boy came home late last night. He was out of breath and looked like he'd seen a ghost."

"What was he doing out so late and why don't I remember any of this?"

She smiles. "Probably because you were fast asleep on the sofa snoring at the TV."

I scratch the chin of my two-day-old beard. "Did you ask him what he was doing out so late?"

"Of course, I did."

"What did he say?" I ask, hearing the impatience reflected in my voice.

"He told me he wanted to see the fireflies one last time before heading back to the city."

"Did he say anything else?"

I see the look of concern. "No, he just said he was tired, and then he ran upstairs before I could ask another question."

"Do you think he saw something?'

"I don't know for sure, Abe. But I reckon it would be best if you speak to him before his momma picks him up later this morning."

I take a deep breath and let the air out slowly through my nose.

"Is he up yet?"

"I heard him flush the toilet, but he hasn't come downstairs yet."

"Okay. When he comes down for breakfast, send him out here and I'll speak to him."

She nods, drinks the last of her coffee and says, "I guess I better get breakfast started. Can I get you another cup of coffee?"

I shake my head. "No thank you, but maybe later. Right now, I just want a little quiet to think about what I'm going to say."

Dell takes my hand, bends over, and kisses me on the lips. "You're a good Grandpa, Abe, and I'm sure you'll come up with a good explanation for whatever he asks you."

I can't help but smile at her misplaced faith in my good judgment. Right now, I'm hoping that the boy saw nothing unusual and that Dell is mistaken about the look she saw on his face last night.

I close my eyes for a moment and ask the good Lord to give me the strength and wisdom to find the right words to convince my grandson that he didn't see what he thinks he saw.

Jesus, Abraham, you're getting way ahead of yourself. For all you know you're making a big deal out of nothing.

"Grandpa?" I hear a voice in the darkness.

I open my eyes and Joshua is standing in front of me. A blonde haired, blue-eyed, baby-faced teenager who is the spitting image of his daddy, God rest his soul.

"Good morning, Son. Did you sleep okay?"

Joshua doesn't look me in the eye when he answers. "Sure, Grandpa. I slept just fine."

I've known my grandson long enough to know when he's lying.

"Well, that's good to hear. I need you to stay sharp for the drive back."

Joshua smiles and says, "You know I don't drive yet, Grandpa."

"I know that" I say winking at him, "but you know there are a lot of crazy drivers out there, and I need you to help your momma keep an eye on the road."

"I'll do my best."

"Good boy."

"Anyway, Grandma told me to come get you, because breakfast is almost ready."

"Great, but before we go inside, I'd like to talk to you about something. Why don't you have a seat?"

Joshua sits down and stares out into the distance.

"Grandma told me you got home late last night."

"Yes, sir."

"She said something about you going out to the woods to see the fireflies."

"Yes, sir."

"Did you see what you went to see?"

Joshua shifts his weight in the seat. "I did and they were beautiful."

"Not something that you'll ever see in the city."

"No, sir."

"Grandma also told me that when you got home last night you looked like you'd seen a ghost." I chuckle and ask, "Did you?"

Joshua looks away again and swallows hard. "I don't really want to talk about it Grandpa. Can we just go eat?"

"I know when something is bothering you, Son, and I really don't want you leaving the farm without telling me the truth. You know that you can tell your Grandpa anything?"

Joshua turns to face me and I see a look of uncertainty.

"If I tell you, you'll only laugh at me. You'll think I'm being silly."

"Try me. I promise I won't laugh or think you're silly," I reply with a smile.

"I know you won't believe this, but I was waiting to see the fireflies, and all of a sudden there was this really weird noise, and then this super-bright light, and it was hanging right over the forest. And then I heard – I'm sure it was footsteps, Grandpa! And then..."

"You what? What did you see?"

He swallows hard again like his throat has gone dry, but he manages to say, "I saw eyes, Grandpa. A whole bunch of green eyes, staring at me through the trees!"

"What did you do?" I ask, trying to hide my concern.

He gives me a look that says, Are you kidding me? What kind of a dumb question is that? But out loud he says, "I ran! I ran like hell and I didn't stop until I got back here!"

Oh crap. It's worse than I thought. What now? What do I tell him now?

Then suddenly the answer comes to me and I burst out laughing, then slap my knees and laugh even louder.

I see a surprised and hurt look, and he cries out, "You promised you wouldn't laugh! You promised, Grandpa."

He stands up to leave, but I grab his arm and pull him back down to his chair.

"Wait, let me explain. I'm not laughing at you; I'm laughing at myself.... at something similar that happened to me when I was just a few years older than you."

Joshua stares at me as if he didn't know what to make of my comment. "Are you telling me that you think you saw a UFO too?"

"Well, sort of. Let me explain."

"I'm listening."

"I was out fishing one day, standing knee-deep in a cold stream at my favorite fishing spot. Two hours in, and nothing— not a single fish. That was really odd because that place was usually a sure thing, but not that day.

"I was feeling pretty lousy about it, but then all of a sudden I forget all about the fish. The darn ground was starting to shake!

"So, I backpedal to the shoreline as fast as I can go, thinking to myself, 'What in tarnation is this? It's been more than thirty years since the last earthquake hereabouts!'

"I just barely made it to the shore when there's a huge 'Boom!' and the ground rips right open, just a few yards away from me. This massive jet of hot water and steam shoots into the air; the ground just keeps right on shaking and the rip gets wider and wider.

"Then this big oblong thing starts rising up from the steam, and it's hovering right in the air. Then it starts to spin and flash like what you kids nowadays call a disco ball, and this weird contraption starts coming out of it, something like a large telescope. The thing shoots out a big red beam, going around and around in a circle until it spots me.

"Every impulse in my body was telling me to run, but I couldn't move. The red beam got brighter and brighter and brighter; suddenly this blast of energy hits me and sends me flying backwards.

"Next thing I know, I'm opening my eyes. The weird thing is gone, the hole in the ground closed up like it was never there, and the hot sun is shining in my face. That's when I realized what had happened.

"Staring at me wide-eyed, Joshua asks, "What happened?"

"Well, Son, as I sat up and rubbed my eyes, I laughed and said to myself, no more 50s sci-fi movies and Jack Daniels the night before a fishing trip!"

Joshua has a look of disbelief. "Grandpa, you made that up."

"No, I swear it's true. I believed every moment of it while it was happening."

"But that didn't actually happen to you. You were drunk."

"Exactly!"

"But that's not the same thing that happened to me. I wasn't drunk. I saw what I saw."

I smile at him and say, "I know you weren't drunk, but are you sure you saw what you think you saw? On a dark night, in a dark forest with a full moon, wiser and older men than you have sworn they've seen crazy things."

I see a shadow of doubt, so I continue, "Are you sure you didn't get there early and laid down on the grass and dozed off waiting for the fireflies to appear?"

"I, ah, did lay on the grass, but I... I don't think I fell asleep?"

I smile. "Hmm. If these things with green eyes were out there, why didn't they chase you all the way home?"

I see more doubt reflected in his eyes as he shakes his head. "I don't know."

"Grandma and I have lived on this farm for over forty years; don't you think we would have noticed something as strange as what you describe?"

"I... I guess so." Joshua stares up at me and I see a look of hesitation in his eyes.

"What is it, boy? Whatever it is, say it."

He points at my forehead and asks, "Grandpa, what happened to your temple? How did you get that scar?"

I'm ready for this one. "Well, boy, a few months back I had an odd growth on my left temple, so I had it tested and it turns out it was cancerous, so it had to be removed." I see the look of concern on Joshua's face. "Nothing to worry about, Son, they caught it in time and everything is fine. All that's left is this little scar."

I stand up and place my hand on his shoulder. "Come on, Son, let's go eat breakfast before it gets cold."

"What about Grandma?"

"What about her?" I reply.

"I notice that she has a scar in exactly the same place. Did she get cancer too?"

Damn it, I think, *I told Della to keep that scar covered with makeup while the Boy was visiting. Think fast, Abe!*

"Cancer? No, don't be silly. Grandma slipped on a wet step and hit her forehead on the railing. It was a pretty nasty cut, so I had to run her up to the doctor for stitches. She's fine now."

Joshua grins and says, "Strange how the scars are both in the same place. What are the chances of that happening?"

"Well, to be truthful, Boy, they aren't exactly in the same place or even the same size, but it is kinda freaky."

Joshua stands up. "Sure, Grandpa, whatever you say."

I wink at him. "Ah, the story about me and the Jack Daniels… Grandma doesn't know about that and I'd like to keep it that way."

Joshua smiles and runs two fingers across his mouth as if zipping his lips. "Your secret is safe with me."

"Also, please don't ask Grandma about her scar, she's still really embarrassed about slipping and hurting herself. It makes her feel like she's getting old."

"Will do, Grandpa."

"Good boy," I say, tossing my fingers through his hair as we walk towards the door.

Joshua stops in his tracks and turns towards me. "I have one more confession."

Oh no, what now? I think.

"I took one of the horses and rode past the old barn in the north field last week."

I squint and raise my voice louder then I mean too. "I thought I told you to stay away from that old barn!"

He gets a frightened and apologetic look. "I wasn't planning to go anywhere near the barn, I swear, but while I was riding through the field I smelled something awful. It smelled so gross that it made me gag, and it was coming from the old barn. I didn't get close but I was close enough to notice the deadbolt on the barn door."

"Raccoons," I blurt out. "We had an infestation of raccoons in that old barn, so I set some traps with poison. It must have done the job, but I haven't had the chance to clean up the mess. I was waiting until you left."

"Oh, I guess that makes sense."

I can see by the curious look, that there's more. "What else is on your mind? You might as well get it all out in the open."

"Why are all those cars and pickup trucks parked under the trees at the corner of the east field?"

"You managed to ride all the way out to the corner of the east field," I say, trying to keep my disapproval from showing in my voice. "I haven't been out there in years, nor have I used it for cattle or farming, so I rent it out to a friend of mine who owns an auto parts store and scrap yard. He pays me to park his cars there."

I see the incredulous look. "Wow, scrap yard? Some of the cars look like they're still in great condition, some even look brand new."

"Appearances can be deceiving from a distance. Most of those cars are no longer roadworthy and have been gutted for parts. They are mostly hollow shells."

"Oh," is all he says, but I'm not sure he believes me.

He sees the hurt look, so I use it to my advantage by saying, "You don't look like you believe me? Do you think that I would lie to you?"

He shakes his head, "No, sir; I believe you."

"Good. You wouldn't want to hurt my feelings, would you?"

He smiles and says, "No, Grandpa."

The look on his face is sincere and I breathe a sigh of relief.

"Alright, let's go inside, wash up and have breakfast."

As the boy goes to wash up, I reassure Della that everything is going to be just fine.

"I think I addressed all of his concerns, but it's probably good that he's leaving today."

I see the sadness in her eyes, so I reach out and hug her. "I know, I hate it too."

Since it will be the last breakfast we will have with the boy for the foreseeable future, Dell has gone all out and made all of Joshua's favorites, including hotcakes, country bacon, sweet ham, and a large serving of scrambled eggs.

I laugh as I watch the boy suck down the food like a vacuum cleaner; I'd forgotten how much food a teenager can consume.

After breakfast Joshua goes up to his room to finish packing while Dell and I clear the table and wash the dishes.

Dell, elbow deep in soapy water, asks me, "Do you think the boy believed you?"

"I can't say for sure, but I think so."

"What if he talks? What if he says something to Jeanine?"

"I don't think he'll say anything to his momma, but I'll talk to him again before she gets here."

"But what if—"

I interrupt her. "Dell, I don't think he will. But if he does, there's not much we can do about it... is there?"

"Last thing we need is people snooping around here—"

"Stop! Stop worrying. You knew that someday this could happen. Maybe it's for the best. We ain't getting any younger."

"What about the community? They will wreak havoc on all our friends and their families. Can we live with that?"

I shrug my shoulders. "It doesn't feel any better doing it to total strangers—does it?"

She nods in acknowledgement, and I see moisture glisten in the corner of her eyes. Defeated and dejected she goes back to washing the dishes. It breaks my heart to see her this way, but what can we do? Hopefully, the good Lord will forgive us.

My unpleasant thoughts are interrupted by the sound of a car horn.

"That must be Jeanine."

Dell smiles, wipes her hands on the dish towel and runs out to greet our daughter. I stay behind waiting for Joshua to come down. Seconds later he runs down the stairs lugging his suitcase.

I wrap my arms around him and say, "I guess this is it."

He hugs me tight. "I'm going to miss you, Grandpa."

"Me too, Boy," I say, holding back the tears.

"I'll still come and visit when I get a chance."

"I hope so." But I know it is highly unlikely, now that he and Jeanine are moving across the country to New York City. "I want you to study hard and do well at school."

"I will, Grandpa."

"Good boy," I say as I release him. "I also need you to promise me that you won't say a word to your momma about what we spoke about this morning. She's already upset with me and I don't want her to hate me any more than she already does."

I see the sadness. "She doesn't hate you Grandpa, I won't let her."

"Thank you, Son. That means a lot to me." I say placing my hand on his shoulder. "You best be going... don't keep your momma waiting."

"Why don't you come outside and say hello?" he says with a pleading tone in his voice.

"Your Grandma will say goodbye for the both of us," I say, pushing the screen door open and guiding him outside.

"Bye, Grandpa. Thanks for everything."

"Get going now. You don't want to see a grown man cry."

Joshua walks out onto the porch and I let the screen door close behind him. Jeanine and Dell turn to stare at me. Jeanine looks me in the eye, but she says nothing. She is definitely her father's daughter.

This farm has been in our family for three generations, and because of my selfish daughter, this legacy will end with me. I know that I should forgive her and move on—she has—but the stubborn old fool in me can't seem to let it go.

After what's happened the last few years, a part of me is glad to let the farm go, and in a sad way, I'm happy that she and the boy are moving as far away from here as possible.

I watch as the car doors slam and the car backs up. As it begins to pull away, Joshua sticks his head out of the window and yells, "I love you, Grandpa!"

I feel the lump in my throat, wave and whisper, "I love you too, boy." Then the tears begin to fall.

I watch as the car disappears down the long dirt driveway leading to the main road.

I quickly wipe my eyes before Dell gets back in the house. But when I open the screen door, I see the tears and wrap my arms around her.

Be strong, I think, as I hug her tightly.

"She will be fine. They both will," I say, trying to reassure her.

"I know, but it's still hard to see my babies go. I will miss them so much."

We stand in our embrace for a few more minutes until there is no longer a reason to. Then I place my arm around Dell's shoulder. "I guess we better get back to work."

Out of nowhere a sharp pain strikes my left temple and I hunch over. Instinctively I rub my scar. A couple of seconds later, the same thing happens to Dell. The pain is agonizing, but fortunately brief. It will come and go for the rest of the day unless we give them what they need.

Dell dries the tears with her sleeve and nods in acknowledgement.

"Dell, you load the shotguns while I drive up to the main road with the sign."

She kisses me on the cheek. "Okay, sweetheart, be careful."

I jump into our old pickup truck and drive the quarter mile to the main road. I take the sign out of the bed of the truck and lean it against the fence post.

The sign reads, TODAY ONLY - FREE EGGS, FREE MILK.

I get back into the truck, put it in gear and head back to the farmhouse. The cool breeze coming through the cab window of the truck feels good against my face. I shouldn't smile, but I can't help myself when I think that there are still people in this world who believe that you can get something for nothing. I guess some people learn the hard way that there is no such thing as a free lunch.

I reach the farmhouse and step out of the truck. Dell is waiting on the porch, sitting in her rocker with a shotgun across her lap.

"Everything all set?" she asks as I sit down in my chair beside her.

"Yes. And now we wait."

She clears her throat. "Hopefully not too long. I think our visitors are getting restless."

"Yup! It's time to feed the Godless Vermin."

Out of the corner of my eye I see dirt flying in the air as a car appears in the distance.

A part of me whispers, "Turn around, you damn fool," but I know they won't.

Although we can't see them or hear them, deep within the forest, creatures with green eyes are staring between the trees, lusting for dinner to be served.

Words to a Kill

2018 Finalist in the Royal Palm Literary Awards Competition
(Short Story Genre)

Marco and his older brother Sonny meet every Sunday at Carmelo's Italian Cafe to discuss sports and business and to bullshit about friends and family.

Something is different this Sunday. Marco notices that he is doing all the talking, while his brother just sits there nodding his balding head and sipping his espresso.

"What's bugging you, Sonny? You got trouble with the business?"

Sonny owns a chain of Italian Deli's scattered throughout the New York City area.

"Nah, business is good and profits are up. I'm thinking about expanding into Jersey."

"Then what is it? You ain't hardly said a boo this morning."

Sonny lifts his arm to get the server's attention, then raises his voice. "Hey, Carmen! Can we get two more espressos and a couple of cannoli?"

"Sure, Salvatore. Coming right up," the waitress says.

Sonny strokes his unshaven face and stares out the window.

"Jesus, Sonny, you're giving me the creeps," Marco says. "What the hell is wrong? I didn't think there was anything we couldn't talk about."

"It's Lucy. She's driving me crazy!"

"What?" Marco stares at his brother.

"What, what?" Sonny throws his hands up in the air. "Are you deaf? Didn't you hear what I said?"

Marco is about to reply but stops himself when he sees Carmen coming toward their table with the coffee and cannoli. He takes a sip from the espresso cup she puts in front of him and waits until she walks away. "What about Lucy?"

"I told you, she's driving me fucking crazy."

"Come on, Sonny, tell me something I didn't already know. You've been saying that for years."

Sonny wipes sweat from his forehead. "It's gotten worse than ever. Since her car accident she's become a basket case."

"I know she don't drive no more."

"I got no problem with that. I don't mind doing all the driving. I just wish she'd shut the hell up and behave herself in the car."

"I ain't following you, Sonny."

"Since her crash, she's become a front seat Nazi. Shouting out orders, giving me directions, pointing out everything I'm doing wrong. As far as she's concerned, I can't do anything right. You'd think that after thirty stinking years without an accident, she'd trust my driving, but shit no, the way she screams at me you'd think that I'm working towards my learner's permit."

Marco begins to giggle but stops when he sees the scowl on his brother's face.

"This ain't funny. If she keeps shooting her mouth off at me, I'm liable to smack her."

"You ain't never hit Lucy."

"I came real close a couple of days ago," Sonny says. He shifts uncomfortably in his seat.

"What happened?"

"I'm driving down Front Street and some *strunz* cuts me off, happens all the time. My Lucy gets absolutely hysterical and starts screaming at me as if it was my damn fault."

"I'm sure she just got spooked. It's only been two months since her accident, Sonny. What do you expect? When I think about how close she came to cashing in, it gives me chills inside," Marco says, looking to the heavens and making the sign of the cross.

"Who the hell's side are you on?"

"I ain't on nobody's side. I'm just saying—"

Sonny cuts his brother off before he can finish his sentence.

"That ain't the worst of it. When I catch up to the *stugots* at the next light, my wife rolls down her window, gives him the finger and tells the guy to go fuck himself. Thank God, the guy didn't get out of his car, because he looked like a big SOB, but he rolls down his window, looks me straight in the eye and says, 'Hey buddy, tell your bitch to shut up or I'll do it for you.' Lucy was about to say something when I reached over and covered her mouth with my hand."

"Jesus. I can't believe she said that."

Sonny swallows hard and says, "I wish I could say that it was the first time she's done that, but it ain't. It's like she's looking to get me beat up!" He looks around and lowers his voice. "You know I ain't no coward, Marco, but the way things are today you never know when someone's packing a gun, and I ain't got no death wish. You know what I'm saying?"

Marco takes a deep breath and lets the air escape through his teeth. "What did you say to Lucy?"

"When the guy pulled away from the light, I turn to her and lose it. I start screaming at her, asking her what the hell is wrong with her. 'You wanna get us both killed?', I say. She looks at me with this crazy stare and says, 'I didn't realize I married such a momma's boy, a damn pussy.' So, I make a fist and go like this,"— he raises his arm in a punching motion—"and I swear, Marco, I was *this* close to belting her in the mouth. The only thing that stopped me was the look on her face—total shock."

Marco stares at his brother as if he's mesmerized. "Holy crap, this doesn't sound good."

"Next thing I know, she starts sobbing and telling me what a disgrace I am. She slaps my arm and says, 'What kind of man beats his wife but refuses to defend her life and honor when it's threatened?'"

"Oh, *Madonna mia*! She really said that?"

"I felt like such a scum bag, Marco. We drove the rest of the way home without saying another word."

Marco's eyes shift to the side, and he crumbles the last bit of cannoli under his fingers. "Oh man. If you still love her you gotta fix this, Sonny!"

"Whaddaya mean if I still love her? She's my wife, of course I love her. The problem is that right now, I don't like the way she's treating me and I don't understand why she's acting this way." He rubs his face with his hands. "This is what's got me all confused. When we got home that day, I was feeling pretty low and seriously thinking about getting on my knees and apologizing to her. When I told her I was sorry, she looked at me and said,

'Sorry about what?' Then she acts like nothing happened." Sonny puts his right elbow in his left hand, pinches together the thumb and fingers of his right hand and shakes it in Marco's face. "Only *una pazza* acts like that."

"Aren't you overreacting? I don't think your wife's a crazy person, and neither do you."

"When you hear what she asked me to do next, you might change your mind."

"Did she ask you to take driving lessons?"

"No, smart ass. She asked me if we can go visit Julia and the grandchildren in Savannah."

"So, what's wrong with going to see your daughter?"

"Nothing. I'd love to see Julia and the grandkids, but Lucy doesn't want to fly, she wants me to *drive* her down there."

"So?"

Sonny takes a bite of his cannoli. "*Chooch*, haven't you been listening to a word I said? There's no way our marriage could survive a twelve-hour car ride to Savannah, especially the way she's been acting lately. I'm beginning to think she just likes pushing my buttons and messing with me."

"Come on. Why would she do that? Did you do something you're not telling me about?"

Sonny shifts in his seat. "I swear I ain't done nothing wrong."

"I hope not. You know her family background. The apple don't fall far from the tree."

"When I married her, she swore she wanted nothing to do with her family's Mafioso dealings. She gave all that up for me and the kids."

"Then why would she act this way? Why do I have the feeling there's something you ain't telling me?"

"I told you I ain't done nothing to make her act this way. I don't know why she's behaving the way she is. Maybe it's because she's lost her mind . . . you know, one too many blows to the head from the accident."

"I don't think it's that."

"You don't?" Sonny taps nervously on the table. "Then by all means enlighten me."

"Two weeks ago, when you were on another one of your trips to Italy, *meeting with your suppliers*, I stopped by Lucy's to make sure she was okay and to see if there was anything she needed."

"Hmmm. That's interesting."

"What's interesting?"

"Lucy never mentioned you stopping by the house."

"She probably didn't tell you that I took her grocery shopping, to the mall and to see her sister in upstate New York. We even went out to dinner a couple of nights."

Sonny shakes his head and says, "She didn't tell me nothing about that, but it was awfully nice of you to look after her while I was gone."

"You're welcome. I was just trying to be a good brother."

"Okay. What's the point you're trying to make?"

"My point is that she didn't seem upset or stressed out when I drove her around town. She never raised her voice once."

"Well, ain't that wonderful," replies Sonny. "What are you trying to say?"

"Don't get mad at me for saying this, but is it possible that maybe you drive a little recklessly when she's in the car?"

"What the hell are you talking about? I drive the way I've always driven. She's the one that's changed. I've been driving her around for twenty-five years and she's never had these outbursts in the past."

"Things are different now. Maybe you oughta try driving slower and being more understanding when she's in the car with you."

Sonny looks at his brother and bursts out laughing.

"Oh my God, that's hilarious, Marco. It would take the patience of Job to keep me from strangling her on the twelve-hour drive from New York to Savannah. Do you have any idea how much shit I'm gonna have to put up with on a trip like that?"

"What choice do you have? She's obviously reaching out to you, hoping that a long drive will somehow bring the two of you closer together and perhaps help her get over her anxiety of being in the car with you."

Sonny puts his hand to his chest. "*Madonna mia*, you're giving me indigestion. Since when did my little brother become a fucking shrink?"

"I ain't no shrink, I'm just trying to help you out."

"Well think of something else, because after all these years I ain't gonna change the way I drive."

They order another round of espresso and sit quietly sipping their drinks. Suddenly, Marco puts his cup down and snaps his fingers.

"I think I got an idea!"

Sonny rolls his eyes.

"Remember when cousin Bruno was a young punk hanging out with the wrong crowd?" Marco says. "He was always getting into trouble with the law."

"Yeah, so?"

"Remember how Aunt Rosie put him in the Scared Straight Program and they made him visit Attica Prison, so he could see the harsh reality of prison life from the perspective of the inmates? He was a good boy after that experience."

Sonny smiles. "Are you saying I should take Lucy to some nut house and show her what will happen if she continues acting the way she is?"

"Ha, ha, very funny. But that ain't what I'm talking about."

"You're not making any sense, Marco. What does the Scared Straight Program have to do with this situation?"

"What I'm trying to say is that maybe Lucy can be scared into changing her behavior."

"How do you propose I do that?"

"Maybe we can set up a sting. Well, sting probably ain't the right word, but hear me out. What if we get someone to come after you the next time she goes off and starts cursing another driver?"

"Okay, maybe I'm the *chooch* here, because I have no idea what you're talking about."

Marco lays out this elaborate plan involving a staged incident where some guy cuts Sonny and Lucy off on the way home.

"When Lucy starts cursing and threatening the other driver, the guy pulls a gun and forces you off the road. Once he pulls you over he asks you to step out of the car and begins pistol whipping you and threatens to hurt both of you. Then he puts the gun against Lucy's forehead and asks her to apologize or he'll kill both of you. You beg the guy not to shoot Lucy and offer him money to forget about the whole mess. The guy accepts the money and drives away. Lucy realizes how close you both came to getting killed because of her antics. She now understands that you were right, she needs to keep her anger inside or next time she might get both of you killed. What do you think?"

Sonny gives Marco a deadpan look.

"Great, so she'll stop being aggressive towards other drivers and focus on making my life a living hell instead."

"I think she'll be more understanding because you actually saved her life."

"Jesus, Marco. I think you've been watching to many wise guys movies."

"You got any better ideas? At least think about it."

Sonny looks at his watch and says, "Okay, I'll think about it, but right now I gotta go. I need to fire one of my managers at my Queens store. The *goomba's* been stealing me blind."

"Sorry to hear that."

Sonny throws ten bucks on the table and slaps Marco on the back.

"See you next Sunday, little brother."

"*Ciao,* Salvatore."

Marco watches Sonny leave, then pulls out his cell phone and hits a number on speed dial.

* * *

Three days later Marco's cell phone rings. It's Sonny on the line.

"What's up?"

"She went and did it again. This time to a blue hair and a cop."

"You gotta be kidding. What happened?"

"On Monday we're driving home from the grocery store and this old lady in a Buick drifts into our lane. I'm not sure what she was doing, but she probably didn't see me in her side mirror and her car crossed the white line. Luckily, I noticed she was drifting, so I slowed down and honked my horn. When I pulled up beside the old woman, I could see her trying to apologize to us, but Lucy would have none of that."

"Don't tell me she told the lady to go eff herself?"

"No. But she gave her the middle finger and told her to drop dead. You should have seen the look on the woman's face. I thought she was gonna start bawling."

"Wow. That's pretty harsh."

"This from someone who thinks I should be more understanding towards my wife's crazy-ass stunts."

"What happened with the cop?" Marco asks.

"That was the next day. I'm driving down Anderson Street on my way home from picking Lucy up after physical therapy, when this cop pulls me over. I turn to Lucy and say, please don't say a word. I'll handle this."

"On second thought, I'm not sure I want to know what happened with the cop."

"You won't believe this, Marco. The cop pulled me over to tell me I gotta taillight out on the left side. He gives me a warning and says I need to get it fixed as soon as possible. I thank him and as he begins to walk away, Lucy says real loud and angry, 'I can't believe these cops nowadays. They have nothing better to do than pull over innocent people for a bad taillight. Don't they have murderers, or child molesters to catch? It's pathetic, I tell you.'"

"Oh shit! I can't believe she said that."

"How do you think I felt? I look in my side mirror and watch the cop stop, turn around, and come back to the window. 'License and registration,' he says."

"He gave you a ticket for a stinking taillight?"

"Nope. He told me I was driving over the speed limit, but he was gonna let it slide until my wife opened her big mouth. I was so pissed, Marco."

"I can just imagine. What did Lucy say?"

"I asked her what the hell was wrong with her, and all she did was laugh, which pissed me off even more. Then she has the nerve to say that she was only telling the cop what I was already thinking but was too much of a coward to say to his face."

"Jesus, Sonny. You gotta real problem on your hands. What are you gonna do?"

"I've been thinking about what you said last Sunday. How exactly would that work?"

"Let me talk to a guy I know and see if I can set something up. Can you meet me at Carmelo's tonight and we can talk about it then?"

Sonny is silent for a few seconds, then laughs and says, "Don't get all *Mission Impossible* on me. Why can't you just tell me over the phone right now?"

"What's this *Mission Impossible* shit? All I'm trying to do is help you out and I ain't got all the answers worked out yet. Besides, it's not something I wanna talk about over the phone. You gotta problem with that?"

"Alright, Marco. Don't get so damn defensive about it. I'll meet you tonight at eight. The cannoli are on you, brother."

"Sure. Whatever you say. See you then."

* * *

Sonny arrives at Carmelo's promptly at 8:00 p.m., but Marco is late. He orders a cappuccino and waits. Marco arrives twenty minutes later and drops down in the seat across from him.

"Nice of you to join me," says Sonny in a sarcastic tone. "What the hell took you so long?"

"I found a guy willing to do the job, but he wants three thousand bucks."

"Three thousand bucks! This oughta be good. What exactly are we paying him to do?"

"Rough you up a bit," says Marco, laughing.

"Okay. What am I missing here? Tell me again how your plan is gonna work."

"Aldo is going to be Lucy's next victim."

"Who's Aldo and how do you know him?"

"Aldo is this two-bit punk who moved here from Philly. He's been coming to my barber shop for a trim every couple of weeks for the last six months. Tries to act like a tough guy but he seems really nice to me."

"You trust this guy?"

"He's willing to play the part for three thousand bucks, and Lucy don't know him. What else is there to say?"

"I don't know about this."

"Would you feel better if we arranged to meet somewhere and you can talk with him face to face?"

"Maybe, but you still haven't told me how this whole thing is gonna work?"

Marco slaps him on the back. "That's why I'm here, brother. Let me order an espresso and some tiramisu and I'll tell you what I've come up with, then you can decide if you think it'll work."

Sonny scratches his head and shrugs. "I guess."

The waitress puts Marco's order in front of him, and he plunges his spoon into the brown-sprinkled top of the dessert. "Okay. Here's what I'm thinking. We need to pick a day, place, and time where you'll be driving Lucy somewhere."

"I take her to the hairdresser every other Friday at three-thirty."

"That's great. Where's her salon at?"

"Walton and 5th Street."

"Isn't there an old box factory near there?"

"Yeah, it's been closed for years."

"That's perfect. Nice and deserted."

"Perfect for what?"

"That's the perfect place for Aldo to cause a scene and get Lucy excited. When Lucy starts in on him, Aldo will force you to pull over and you drive into the parking lot of the box factory."

"What if Lucy doesn't bite?"

"Why would she keep her mouth shut now?"

"Good point! But what if she doesn't?"

"Then we call it off and try some other time using someone else."

"So, Aldo gets three thousand bucks for nothing?"

"No. He gets fifteen hundred. Half upfront, the other half if Lucy takes the bait."

"Okay. I guess that's fair. What then?"

"Like I said, when Lucy lays into him verbally, he forces you to pull over and you get out of the car."

"Why the hell would I get out of the car?" asks Sonny. "I never have before."

"Because Aldo has a gun pointed at your head."

"What? No fucking way."

"For Pete's sake, it ain't gonna be loaded, it's just there to scare Lucy." Marco is starting to look frustrated.

"I don't like no gun pointed at my face."

"What would you have him do? Point a finger in your face? That should scare the hell out of Lucy!"

"Fine. He can use the unloaded gun. Then what happens?"

"Aldo walks you to the back of the car, where he sucker punches you in the gut—well, pretends to—and you drop to the ground. Then he pretends to kick you a few times and tells you that your bitch is next. You need to play this up by grunting as if you're hurt and telling him that your wife didn't mean it. That she's sick in the head and sorry about what she said. Then you beg him not to hurt her and promise him money if he lets this go. This is where you give him the other fifteen hundred you owe him. Aldo takes the money and drives away."

Sonny puts his hand up in a "stop" gesture. "I don't know. This sounds a bit kooky to me."

"Hey, I ain't forcing you to do anything you don't wanna do. We can just stop right now and forget about the whole thing."

Sonny rubs his face and lets out a deep breath. "You really think this is gonna work?"

"I think it's gonna scare the crap out of Lucy and hopefully make her think twice before shooting her mouth off. There's no guarantee it'll work, but I think it's gotta good chance."

"What if Lucy wants me to call the cops and give them a description of Aldo? What then?"

"Aldo will be in disguise and the red Dodge Dart he'll be driving will have fake plates. Anyway, I think Lucy will be so scared that she won't recall much of what's happened."

"Maybe you should ask Aldo to threaten to come looking for us if we say anything to the police."

Marco's face breaks out in a smile. "Brilliant idea, brother. Now you're getting into the spirit of this."

Sonny sits quietly for a moment, as if he's contemplating the scam and wondering if it can really work. He finally shrugs his shoulders. "Okay. Let's do this. Just remember, if Lucy ever finds out about this, I'm gonna kick your ass."

"Ooh, Mister Tough Guy! Lucy ain't ever gonna know about this. I'll set everything up and call you on Friday morning. Capish?"

"Fine. Just don't screw this up."

They knock fists and Marco says, "I gotta go."

They laugh, then hug and say goodbye.

* * *

It's three o'clock on Friday. Sonny got Marco's phone call that morning, letting him know that everything is all set, so here he is driving Lucy to her hair appointment.

As he turns onto Walton Street, he spots a red Dodge Dart in his rear-view mirror; a young guy with greasy black hair flopping over his forehead is behind the wheel.

It's just a couple more blocks to the abandoned box factory, so Aldo needs to make his move soon. Sure enough, he passes Sonny, and then cuts in real close to the front of Sonny's car, forcing him to slam on the breaks and lay on the horn.

Lucy jumps. "That son of a bitch came out of nowhere!"

"It's okay. We're fine. Just let it go."

Aldo slows down in front of them as if he is looking for an address. Finally, he comes to a complete stop in the middle of the road and waves at Sonny to pass by him.

Lucy raises her hand. "Can you believe the nerve of this idiot? Apparently, they'll give any *strunz* a driver's license in this state."

As Sonny carefully passes Aldo on the left, Lucy rolls down the window and yells, "Hey asshole! Why don't you get off the road before you cause an accident?"

The guy looks at her, laughs and blows her a kiss.

Lucy is furious. Twisting her head back over her shoulder she yells back at Aldo, "Why don't you take that kiss and shove it up your ass!"

Sonny looks in the rear-view mirror as Aldo guns the engine and whips the Dodge around next to their car. He's got his front passenger window rolled down and a gun pointed at Sonny, his face twisted into a snarl.

"Pull the fuck over!" he screams.

Sonny looks at Lucy. "Now look what you've done! I told you this would happen someday!"

Lucy looks terrified. "Don't stop! Just step on the gas!"

"No way! The guy could just blow my head off right through the window! I'm gonna pull over and see if I can cool him down. Let me handle this."

"Are you out of your mind? Don't you dare stop for this *stonato*!"

"Don't tell me what to do! You started this goddamn mess and I'm gonna get us out of it, alive!"

Sonny pulls his car into the factory parking lot to a secluded spot that can't be seen from the main road; the red Dodge follows right behind him.

Aldo jumps out of the car and swaggers over. He taps on the window and tells Sonny to step outside, then pulls him by the arm to the rear of the vehicle, grabs him by the collar and shoves him against the trunk of the car. He pushes his large pointy nose in Sonny's face, and his cheap musky cologne gets up Sonny's nose.

"What kind of a chicken shit are you?" Aldo says loudly. "Can't you control the mouth on that bitch?"

"She didn't mean nothing by it," Sonny says, trying to sound scared. "She does that to everyone."

"Well, I ain't fucking 'everyone'!"

"Look, I'm sorry, I really am."

Aldo pulls the gun out from behind his back and hits Sonny across the face with it. Sonny drops to the ground and moans in pain, not needing to pretend.

"What the hell did you do that for?" Then he lowers his voice. "This is supposed to be a fake fight, asshole!"

Aldo smirks and kicks Sonny in the side, hard. Sonny cries out, but Aldo kicks him over and over again. Sonny screams for him to stop. Aldo looks at Lucy through the rear window and says with a grin, "You're next, sweetheart!"

"Please stop!" Sonny screams. "Don't hurt my wife! Her mind ain't right, she doesn't know what she's saying!"

Aldo kicks him again and points the gun at his head.

Sonny is feeling the pain from the last kick and begins to wonder whether Aldo is just a bad actor or maybe a little crazy. "Please don't kill us! I have money on me." He pulls the fifteen hundred out of his pocket and waves it in Aldo's face.

Aldo grabs the money, sniffs it, and says, "This is your lucky day, shithead. I'm feeling generous today. I might let you live if you promise to shut your wife up—and don't even think about calling the cops."

"Yes. Yes. We promise!"

As Aldo tucks the gun back in his pants, suddenly a voice rings out.

"Hey *pazzo*! How does *this* feel?"

Lucy is standing by the car holding out a gun. She fires four shots into Aldo's chest. A look of shock spreads over the young man's face, then he crumples to the ground, dead.

"Lucy, what the hell did you do?" Sonny screams. "I had this whole thing under control. You didn't need to shoot anyone."

He drops his head back on the ground and a wave of nausea washes over him. *How could this have gone so wrong?*

Lucy reaches down, picks up Aldo's gun and puts it in her handbag. Then she takes another gun out of her bag, places it in Aldo's hand, and, using his lifeless finger to pull the trigger, shoots Sonny in the stomach and the chest.

Sonny screams in shock. "What the hell?" he groans. "Lucy! You shot me!"

Lucy walks over to Sonny and looks down at his bleeding body. Her voice is cold. "I thought our love would last forever, Salvatore. I remember how happy I was when you married me and promised to love me for the rest of my life. You swore before God and my family that you would love, honor, and cherish me until death do us part."

Sonny begins to cry. "For God's sake, Lucy, I have no idea what you're talking about! Please, honey, call 911. I'm losing feeling in my arms and legs."

"I've been thinking about this for a long time, Salvatore," Lucy says, her face blank. "When you cheated on me before the children were born, I turned the other cheek. I thought that once you became a father you would change your ways. But when I found out about your wife and family in Italy, that was the last straw. You dishonored me, our family and God, and I just couldn't let you get away with that."

Sonny's eyes grow large as he began to cough up blood. "How—did you—find out?" He groans. "She doesn't—mean—anything to—me, Sweetheart. I got her pregnant by—accident, it just happened—and then she—blackmailed me into—marrying her…" His voice gives out.

Lucy's mouth twists in a sneer. "All those monthly business trips to Italy, did you really think I was that stupid? Did you honestly believe you could keep something like this a secret from me? *Disgraziato!*" She takes a tissue out of her handbag and wipes her fingerprints off the gun she used to shoot Aldo.

As Sonny's eyes begin to close, she bends over and places the gun in his hand, wraps his limp finger around the trigger and fires two shots into the distance.

She checks both men for a pulse, then calmly looks in the car to make sure she hasn't left any incriminating evidence, and walks away from the box factory lot, down Walton Street. When she reaches Third Avenue, she pulls out her cell phone and makes a call.

"Hey, it's me."

"Did everything go okay?"

"Everything went as planned."

"I know this is a stupid time to ask, but did you remember to cancel the hair appointment?"

"Of course."

"What about the gun? Did you use the unmarked gun I got for you?"

"I did."

"You don't sound too good."

"After what I just did, you expect me to sound good? I feel like shit."

"Do you feel bad about Sonny?"

Her voice breaks as she says, "No. I feel bad for my children; they didn't know what a scumbag their father was. They'll be devastated when they find out he's dead."

"I don't know what to say, Lucy."

"There's nothing to say. Poor Aldo, I'll never forget the look on his face. He had no idea what was coming. Did he *have* to die?"

"Lucy. We went over this a million times. Why are you questioning this now? Aldo was not a nice guy. He did his share of bad things to innocent people. He left Philly because he owed lots of money to some really nasty *goombas* and he may even have killed a few people along the way. If it hadn't happened today, it would have happened sooner or later. His life was destined to end badly."

"I guess you're right, but it doesn't make this any easier."

"I'm worried about you. You gonna be alright with this?"

"Don't worry, *caro,* I'll be fine. I'm waiting where we arranged; come pick me up. I need to be at home when the call comes. I need to be ready to answer all their questions."

"I'll be there in five minutes."

"I love you, Marco."

"I love you too, Honey."

Tormented Heart

I'm driving through the outskirts of Sebastopol, California, and I arrive at the final bend where Bodega Highway continues through a lush valley filled with apple trees.

The needle on my gas gauge is pointing toward empty, but I don't feel like pumping my own gas, so I stop for fuel at one of the last full-service stations in the area.

"You in town on business or pleasure?" the kid who's pumping the gas asks in a friendly tone, obviously just making conversation.

I'm in no mood for idle chit-chat.

"Neither," I say. I hand him a twenty-dollar bill and pull away from the pump, getting back on the road.

The afternoon sun is shining brightly through the front windshield of my wife's red Toyota Celica GT, reflecting off her wedding band as it twirls on a gold chain dangling from the front mirror.

The late October air smells crisp and sweet as it flows through the open windows and large sunroof. It's a dramatic change from the damp fog and chilly breeze I've left back in San Francisco.

Val would have loved this weather, I think as I fly past the sign denoting the Town of Occidental, next right.

I smile as I recall the hair-raising experience of driving the Bohemian Highway in the dark of night on our first trip to

Occidental. Negotiating the narrow road flanked by tall, dense trees on either side is challenging enough in the light of day; it was downright treacherous in the dark of night. My wife Valerie was always a nervous passenger, but that night she didn't open her eyes until I told her we had arrived safely in Occidental.

Fortunately, the wild drive was all worth it. We enjoyed a wonderful night having an excellent dinner at Negri's Italian Restaurant and later took a stroll along the quiet, picturesque streets of the old railway town. This was a place we would come to love and visit time and time again over the years.

I ease off the gas pedal as I approach the town of Bodega, made famous in the early sixties when Alfred Hitchcock chose to feature some of the local scenery in his cult film *The Birds*.

Val would always say, "This town is so small, if you blink you'd drive right past it." And she was right.

I turn left on Bodega Lane, drive a short distance up the hill and park in front of what was once James E. Potter Elementary School, which is now a privately-owned residence. This old schoolhouse was made famous in the movie, along with the tiny idyllic church with the white steeple known as St. Teresa's.

During the tourist season you can barely find a place to park on this street, but today I'm all alone.

Removing the gold chain from the mirror, I place it around my neck. I pull a small silver vial from my shirt pocket and place it against my lips, then I stand in front of the old schoolhouse trying to snap a selfie using my cell phone. My attempt to smile for the photograph seems sad and contrived, so I settle for just taking the photograph without frowning.

Clutching her wedding band in my hand I think, *This use to be such a wonderful place, but without you, Sweetheart, it's lost its charm and magic.*

I decide to walk up the hill to St. Teresa's Catholic Church, but I hesitate before entering through the beautiful arched doors.

Religion was always Val's thing, I only attended church because I knew it pleased her and giving up one hour of my time once a week seemed like a small price to pay to make her happy. Since her death, I've thought about life after death and I've wondered if I'll ever see my sweet Valerie again. It's the only thing that makes me want to believe.

I walk into the church, go up to the front pew, kneel and stare at the crucifix, praying to a God I hope exists. "God, I don't know what's true and what isn't, but I want to believe, so if my Valerie is up there with you, please send me a sign—any sign." I sit in silence, waiting, but nothing happens.

"If you're up there, Val, I want you to know that I love you and I miss you every d—" My voice breaks as my emotions get a stranglehold on my throat. "If you can hear me sweetheart, then meet me at the Pearly Gates."

I feel like I can't breathe. I know if I don't leave right away, the tears will begin and there'll be no way to stop them. I can't face that crippling pain again, I just can't.

I exit the church and stop outside the front entrance to inhale cool air into my lungs and feel the sunshine on my face. I walk back to the car, return the vial to my pocket and the gold chain to the mirror, and I sit quietly listening to the sound of the birds chirping.

I stare at Val's wedding band. "How many times did we stop here, Val? I'd guess fifty or sixty times over our thirty-six years of marriage."

My reflection in the rearview mirror captures the sad look on my face and the glistening moisture in the corner of my eyes.

Positive thoughts, Austin, don't do this to yourself, I think, trying to distance myself from this sad moment.

I recall how every time we travelled through this part of Sonoma County, Val would insist that we stop here to have our photograph taken in front of the old schoolhouse and church.

I once asked her why we needed to do this every single time.

She smiled and replied, "Life is way too short, Sweetie. You never know when all of this will be gone. What if something happened to this old schoolhouse or, God forbid, to one of us? I know it might sound silly, but I'd hate to miss the opportunity to capture this special moment one last time."

Her words had sounded melodramatic back then, but today I wish nothing more than to hear the sound of her voice and to have her standing next to me, smiling for one more photograph.

The dry lump in my throat tells me I need to leave this place.

It took me three long years to work up the nerve to return to the north coast. I need to finish this for Val, I think as I shove the key into the ignition and start the engine. *For God sake, get the hell out of here before the tears begin flowing and you lose your nerve.*

I coast cautiously down the hill back to the highway. Turning left, I travel slowly through the small town of Bodega and within minutes arrive at the junction of US 1 and Bodega Highway.

Another right-hand turn and I'm heading southwest along US 1 for a few miles, then the highway turns north along the Pacific coast and I reach my final destination, Bodega Bay, California.

Bodega Bay is a picturesque fishing village located on the Pacific coast of northern California. Although there are still a few fisheries in the area, the majority of the people Val and I met over the years were either retired or worked in the hospitality industry catering to the many tourists who frequent the area.

There's a wonderful golf course where Val and I spent many an afternoon playing and enjoying the sunshine, great hotel accommodations and even a campground for the outdoorsy types. There are several fine restaurants some of which we frequented often, featuring fresh caught local seafood, tasty alcoholic drinks, and beautiful sunset views. There are also several cozy little bars, and small quaint shops selling local arts and crafts. Val was a souvenir junkie, so over the years we pretty much stopped at all of the shops in town.

Of course, our favorite place to watch the sunset was at Sonoma Head State Park, on the southern tip of Bodega Bay peninsula. It became a tradition that on the first day of each visit Val and I would buy a bottle of wine, cheese, crackers, Italian sausage, and a jar of antipasto at the Tides Wharf Market, then head over to Sonoma State Park for a sunset picnic.

Heading down the hill into Bodega Bay, I drive past another treasured location in our travel history, Lucas Wharf Restaurant and Bar. This was one of Val's favorite restaurants and the place the locals always recommended.

I have a dinner reservation at Lucas Wharf Restaurant for four o'clock, and I booked a room at The Inn at the Tides Hotel before I left San Francisco. Although I had the feeling that neither would be busy on a weeknight, I made the reservations anyway, just to ensure that this night would be perfect and that our favorite table by the window at Lucas Wharf and our special room at The Inn at the Tides was available.

As I continue north on US 1, I spot the famous landmark sign for The Inn at the Tides, across the street from The Tides

Wharf Restaurant and Market. Both locations were made famous by the Hitchcock movie. The original hotel burnt down in the late sixties and had to be rebuilt. The restaurant and market were renovated and expanded in the nineties.

I pull the car under The Tides Hotel porte-cochere, switch off the engine, reach for the handle to open the door and then hesitate.

It's been three long years since my last visit, and the thought of stepping into the lobby and seeing the familiar faces without Val by my side feels overwhelming. The hotel staff has always been wonderful to us and prides themselves in knowing their frequent guests by name. Val and I stayed at The Tides so often, for so many years, that everyone on the staff knew us.

Years of therapy, soul searching, and countless medications have not made it any easier for me to answer questions about Valerie's death.

Even after three years the memory of the police officers knocking on my door with the horrifying news is still fresh in my mind. I remember the sad and sympathetic look in their eyes as they informed me that my wife had been struck by a drunk driver while crossing the street in downtown San Francisco. She passed away in the ambulance on the way to the hospital.

Come on Austin, you can do this. Open the damn door and get it over with.

I take a deep breath, swing the car door open, get out of the car, and walk up the steps into the hotel lobby.

It smells like freshly baked chocolate chip cookies.

"Oh, my goodness, welcome back, Mr. Drummond," says a woman with a squeaky voice and toothy smile whose face is familiar to me. "It's been such a long time since your last visit! We're so glad to see you again."

"Thank you," I reply, staring down at my watch, trying to avoid eye contact. "I know I'm early, but it's been a long drive and I'm hoping my room is ready?"

She looks at the computer screen, then reaches for a room card and says, "You and Mrs. Drummond are in room 1408, second floor unit, last building at the top of the hill, as per your reservation request. We don't have many guests staying with us, so your building should be nice and quiet tonight."

I hand her my debit card and say, "Wonderful. Thank you again. Where do I sign?"

She places the paperwork in front to me and points. "Sign and initial here. We'll also need the make, model, and license plate number of your vehicle."

"Oh darn. I'm driving my wife's car and I'm not familiar with her license plate number. I'll need to pop outside and check the plates. I'll be right back."

"No rush, Mr. Drummond. Say hello to Mrs. Drummond for me. I assume she fell asleep in the car during the drive up?"

"Yes", I reply. "I'll be right back with that plate number."

"Tell her I said hello. I'm sure I'll see her later."

I politely nod while thinking, *Val is asleep all right, but unfortunately the sleep is an eternal one.*

The Inn at the Tides consists of several buildings scattered up a hillside, almost motel-style, with a gas station at the bottom of the driveway near Highway US 1. Each two-story building has several rooms with private entrances to the outdoors.

It's just before three o'clock when I settle into my room and unpack my clothes. I set the urn holding Valerie's ashes on the mantel over the fireplace right next to the complimentary bottle of Salmon Creek Chardonnay.

It was in this very room, twenty years ago, that Valerie informed me that she wanted her final resting place to be here. I thought it was the wine speaking, but when she repeated it the next morning at breakfast, I knew she was serious.

I always assumed that we'd be buried together in my family's plot at Holy Cross Cemetery in San Francisco, but Valerie had other plans. I was upset at first, but I knew it was her choice to make. She never agreed to be buried at Holy Cross and made it clear that although she loved me, her dream was to have her body cremated and her ashes scattered off the cliffs of Sonoma Head State Park into the Pacific Ocean.

She was so adamant about this, that she made me swear that I would honor her wishes.

I honestly believed that over time she'd change her mind, but each visit to Bodega Bay seemed to strengthen her resolve. As the years passed, I came to the realization that this would be her final resting place.

My only consolation was that I was several years older than her; I was sure that I'd succumb to the ravages of old age and disease long before her. So, in my mind the sprinkling of her ashes was a moot point.

Yet here I am, I think as I pour myself a glass of wine.

Staring at the urn I raise my glass in a toast. "Here's to you, Sweetheart. It took me a while to get here, but tonight I'm going to fulfill the promise I made to you so many years ago. It's time to set you free, my love."

My voice crumbles at the finality of those words.

I enter the small bathroom, turn on the shower and take off my clothes. As the water rains gently against my tired body, my mind tries to recall Valerie's sweet face. I notice that as the years pass, the stroke of her hand, the scent of her hair, the softness of her skin and the gentle feel of her touch are slowly fading from my memory.

Out of the shower and fully dressed, I place the gold chain with Valerie's wedding band around my neck and slip into my black blazer, the one Valerie loved. She once told me that it made me look like a sexy secret agent. That was many years ago, when I was a strong, confident man with a beautiful and loving wife by my side.

I stare at myself in the mirror, and I don't recognize the thin pale stranger looking back at me. My jacket hangs on my gangly shoulders like on a wooden coat hanger. My face is crisscrossed with deep wrinkles, and my eyes have the look of a man defeated by the ravages of life.

If I stare long enough, I think, *I might just disappear.*

Looking at my watch, I notice that my dinner reservation is in fifteen minutes. Grabbing my wallet and car keys and Val's urn, I head down to the car.

Ten minutes later I'm inside Lucas Wharf Restaurant and Bar, sitting at our favorite table overlooking the Bay. I order the sautéed calamari steak with rice and vegetables, and two glasses of our favorite Chardonnay. I take the small silver vial with some of Val's ashes out of my pocket and lean it against the flower vase. I make a silent toast to our special memories and to a wonderful life well lived.

Some of the customers at the surrounding tables stare at me as if I've lost my mind, while others look at me with sympathy.

The calamari is wonderful as always, but I barely touch my food. I take another sip of wine and ask the server to bring the check.

The sun will be setting soon, and I want to be sure that I don't miss it. When I'm halfway through the parking lot I hear a commotion behind me and look back to see my server running toward me, waving something in his hand.

"Sir! Sir! You left this on the table and I figured it was something important." He holds out his hand, showing me the vial.

"Thank you so much, young man, I can't believe I forgot this. Thank you for saving me the trouble of coming all the way back here to get this later."

"No problem, Mr. Drummond. I hope everything's okay?" the server asks with a genuine look of concern on his face.

"It will be, now that you returned this to me," I reply while reaching into my wallet. "By the way, how do you know my name?"

"That's the name you gave on your reservation, sir."

"Oh, right. I guess I'm not thinking straight. Anyway, please accept this as my way of saying thank you."

The young man's eyes light up when he sees the fifty-dollar note, but immediately begins shaking his head and waving his hands. "No, that's too much, Mr. Drummond. I can't accept that."

"Please... I insist that you take the money." I point to the vial in my hand. "This means the world to me."

"Thank you, sir, and God bless you. This is extremely generous."

"That's nice of you to say, son. Would you mind a piece of advice from an old man?"

The server nods. "Sure."

"Don't ever take anything in life for granted. Live every single day like it was your last. If you're lucky enough to find someone who loves you, don't ever let her go. Remember that you're only here for a limited time. Good luck, young man."

I spot him in my rear-view mirror, standing in the parking lot staring at the fifty-dollar bill, as my car turns onto Highway 1.

I drive north along the highway until I reach Eastshore Road, then turn left and follow Eastshore southwest until it meets Bay Flat Road which then becomes Westshore Road. I drive past Gourmet Au Bay, one of our favorite watering holes. I remember spending many a wonderful evening sipping wine on their outside patio overlooking the marina.

Westshore Road loops around the west side of Bodega Bay ending at Sonoma Head State Park. I have always loved this scenic drive along Westshore Road passing several familiar landmarks like Spud Point Marina, Westshore Regional Park, a few small fisheries, and the entrance to UC Davis – Bodega Marine Laboratory.

Once Westshore Road reaches the state park entrance, I make a hard right and climb the vertical hill toward the Bodega Bay Trail Head.

It's about five thirty so I have plenty of time to park the car and walk south up the steep trail, away from all the prying eyes of visitors who park in the lot and watch the sun set from the seats in their cars.

The wind is noticeably stronger and colder up here, and after walking for ten minutes I stop to catch my breath and stare at the tall grass and brush across the hillside. Val and I have spotted many a buck and doe in this area, but tonight the field is lifeless. The only sound I hear is sea lions barking as they lie on the jagged rock islands nearby.

My hands feel cold against the ceramic urn, but I hold on tight and continue up the trail.

I reach my final destination, walk to the edge of the cliff and drop to my knees as the sun slowly sinks toward the horizon. My eyes fill with tears as each fond memory of my life with Valerie stabs my heart like thorns from a rose. Even in my pain and sadness, I'm struck by the serenity and beauty of my surroundings and I realize why Valerie chose this as her final resting place.

Opening the lid of the urn, I take a handful of Valerie's ashes and scatter them over the cliff. I watch as they fly out toward the vast Pacific Ocean. I take another handful, and I struggle for words to say.

"Goodbye, Sweetheart. You're the best thing that ever happened to me, and since you've been gone I've missed you with every breath I've taken. God speed, my love, fly home, fly away until the day we hopefully meet again."

I open the palm of my hand to release her ashes. But just then the wind shifts, and the ashes fly back at me, landing on my face and clothes. In that moment, I realize Valerie is sending a final goodbye. Once again, I can feel the stroke of her hand, smell the scent of her hair, sense the softness of her touch and the tenderness of her kiss. Perhaps it's just my imagination, but in this moment, I choose to believe what I choose to believe.

I hear myself whisper, "Goodbye, Baby, I've set you free."

Overwhelmed with grief, I fall on my side, curl up in a ball and I cry uncontrollably.

I don't know how long I lie on the cold ground, but by the time I finally return to my hotel room it is after seven o'clock.

I change out of my sports jacket into jeans and a polo shirt, and under the cover of darkness, I go downstairs to the parking lot. There is something I have to do on my car. I guess the lady at the front desk wasn't kidding about me having my own private building tonight, because my car is the only one in the parking lot.

I grab the toolbox and a flashlight from the back seat of the Celica and follow the instructions I downloaded from the internet to my cell phone yesterday.

Ten minutes later, I'm back in my room washing my hands. I locate the envelope I've hidden in the zippered compartment of my overnight bag, pick up the silver vial, and place both in the inside pocket of my black leather jacket.

There's a full moon tonight, so all the stairways and sidewalks running between the scattered hotel buildings are very well lit. The walk downhill to Highway 1 is a steep one, so I'm careful not to stumble on my way down to the road.

I arrive near the bottom of the hill and pass the hotel reception building on the right before reaching the 76 gas station on the left-hand side. Val loved to walk down to the gas station to buy coffee and scratch off lotto tickets. I don't ever remember her winning anything, but I know she enjoyed the thrill of playing.

I reach the road, stand at the crosswalk, and watch for oncoming traffic before crossing the busy highway, then make my way across the parking lot of the Tides Wharf Restaurant & Bar, Gift Shop and Market.

The automatic doors slide open and I walk into the noisy, well-lit building. On my left is the Gift Shop, which sells souvenirs and knickknacks to tourists. To my right is the Market, where you can purchase wine, food and fresh fish caught daily from the fishery next door. I walk past both until I reach the entrance to The Tides Wharf Restaurant and Bar.

The hostess greets me with a big smile. "Good evening, sir. How many in your party?"

I raise my index finger. "Party of one."

"Yes sir," she says, grabbing a menu.

"Any chance I can get a table by the window?"

"Give me one minute and I'll check to see if any are available."

"No problem," I reply.

As I'm waiting I stare at the fresh baked goods in the bakery case and *The Birds* movie memorabilia hanging on the near wall.

A moment later the hostess returns and leads me to a table overlooking the bay.

As she turns to leave, I ask, "Is Sophia working tonight?"

"As a matter of fact, she is. Would you like her to wait on your table?"

"Yes, if it isn't too much trouble?"

"No. No trouble at all."

She hands me the menu and begins reciting the daily specials. I interrupt her. "I've already had dinner. I'm just here for some coffee and dessert."

"Okay. I'll let Sophia know."

While waiting for Sophia, I find myself staring out the normally picturesque window, but it's so dark outside that all I see is a lonely man wearing a leather jacket staring back at me.

During daylight hours you can watch the shrimping and fishing boats moving busily through the channel and be entertained by dolphins and sea lions frolicking in the harbor just outside your window. This is one of the reasons Valerie loved this place. It was where we would sit each morning, enjoy a hearty breakfast, and plan our activities for the day.

My thoughts are interrupted by a familiar voice.

"Mr. Drummond! I can't believe it's really you!"

I look up at Sophia's reflection in the window, then turn to greet her.

"Oh, my goodness," I say, as I stand up to give her a hug, "you're as beautiful as ever, Sophia."

"Thank you, Mr. Drummond. That's so sweet of you to say."

We separate from the hug and she asks, "Where have you been? It seems like forever since I last saw you and Mrs. Drummond. I was beginning to worry that something bad might have—" She stops mid-sentence and stares at the empty chair across the table. "Where's Mrs. Drummond?"

I see the look of confusion and I turn my eyes away.

"Is something wrong?"

I hear panic in the sound of her voice, and I can't bring myself to meet her eyes.

"Can you sit for a minute?"

She nods and slumps into the chair. "I was wondering why you stopped coming."

"There is no easy way to say this. It's taken me years to get here and I'm still having a difficult time talking about it. Please let me say what I have to say, and then I'll try to answer any question you might have. Okay?"

Sophia places a hand over her mouth and nods.

"Three years ago, Valerie was struck and killed by a drunk driver. She never regained consciousness and passed away in the ambulance on the way to the hospital. I'm sorry I didn't tell you sooner, but I've been a mess for several years and I just couldn't talk about it."

Sophia drops her head into her hands and begins to sniffle.

"Oh my god, I'm so sorry, Mr. Drummond. She was the kindest, sweetest lady I ever met. This is awful... I'm stunned. I don't know what to say."

She pulls me out of my chair and I feel her body shaking as she hugs me so tightly that I can barely breathe.

"I'm sorry, Sophia. I hope you know how much she loved you."

"And I loved her too. She was always so sweet to me and my mother. This is what makes this so, so... I'll be right back."

She releases me, wipes the tears on her cheeks, and runs away toward the back of the restaurant.

The restaurant manager must have witnessed the scene because he immediately approaches my table.

"Is there a problem here?"

I explain the situation and he gentle places his hand on my shoulder and gives me his condolences. I watch him leave shaking his head.

I sit quietly, knowing that all eyes in the room are on me and everyone is wondering what the hell I said to make that sweet girl cry.

I stare in the direction where Sophia went, and I think, *I hope she's all right?*

A few minutes later Sophia returns to the table and stands across from me. Her eyes are dry now, but still red-rimmed, and she can't disguise the sad look on her face.

"I can't believe it."

"I'm sorry Sophia. It wasn't my intention to come here and upset you in front of your customers. I'm afraid I've handled this poorly; I've handled everything poorly since Valerie's death."

She takes my hand. "Don't worry about the customers. I'm glad you told me. I'm truly honored to have known her. Thank you for finding the strength to come all this way to let me know."

"You're welcome, sweetheart, but the truth is, I came out here at Valerie's request."

"What do you mean?"

"Valerie made me promise a long time ago that if she passed away before I did, I was to have her body cremated and her ashes scattered over the Pacific Ocean. It took me three years, but I finally fulfilled her wishes today."

A smile spreads across her face and her eyes began to tear up again. "That's so sweet."

"Please stop that or we'll both start crying." I softly pat the back of her hand.

"Okay." She wipes her eyes. "I hope that someday I'll find a love as strong as what you and Mrs. Drummond shared."

"Thank you, Sophia. I have no doubt that someday you'll find your one true love."

"I hope you're right."

"Okay, enough of the tears. So, what does a guy have to do to get a little service around here?"

She gives me a smile and says, "What can I get you, Mr. Drummond? My treat."

"Coffee and apple pie à la mode."

"Coming right up—sir," she replies, giving me a military-style salute.

I pull the silver vial out of my pocket, place it on the table, take a deep breath and whisper, "Wow! That went really well. Didn't it, Val?"

I can almost hear the sound of Valerie's laughter.

Val and I have known Sophia since she was a little girl. Her mother Rosie was a single parent and one of the best servers at The Tides Wharf Restaurant.

Before Sophia began school Rosie couldn't afford to keep her in daycare so she made a deal with the restaurant manager to allow her to bring Sophia to work, as long a Sophia was quiet and behaved herself in the restaurant. Sophia was an incredibly good child and would spend hours in the corner of the restaurant at one of the staff tables playing with her stuffed animals and baby dolls.

Whenever we were in town and visited the restaurant Valerie would make it a point to sit with her and play. After a while a bond grew between them and they became good friends. This continued until Sophia began grade school, then we'd only see her during the summer months.

When Sophia began attending high school she worked at the restaurant on weekends and during her summer break. The last time we saw her she told us that her mother had retired due to arthritic pain in her knees and was on disability.

Back then Sophia also said she was planning on attending college to become a veterinarian.

The sound of the silverware clanking against the table snaps me back to the present.

"Here's your pie and coffee, Mr. Drummond."

"Thank you, Sophia."

She looks at me as if she's going to ask something but hesitates.

I see the concerned look, so I ask, "What is it?"

"I was just wondering, if you're okay, Mr. Drummond? I know it's been a while since I've seen you and you've been through a lot during that time, but..."

I interrupt her before she finishes her thought. "I admit, I've had a rough time since Valerie's death and had some medical issues, that's probably why I've lost so much weight; my hair's gone gray and I look tired. I just had a complete physical about a week ago and my physician gave me a clean bill of health. So, to answer your question – yes, I'm fine."

Trying to change the topic, I ask, "So, how's your mother?"

Her eyes tear up as she gives me a look that says, *You don't know.* "She passed away two years ago."

So much for having brought enough sadness into this day, I think as I feel my throat go dry.

"I'm really sorry to hear that. I had no idea."

"Thank you. I've made peace with her passing. There are times when I really miss her, but I know that she's in a better place."

I wish I felt as certain about my Valerie as you do about your mother.

She pats me on the forearm and says, "The restaurant's getting busy and I have food orders to attend to. Please promise me that you won't leave without saying goodbye."

I grab her hand. "When's your next break? I need to talk to you about something important. There's something I'd like you to have."

"We're short-staffed tonight, so I'm not sure I'll be getting a break anytime soon. I'll tell you what, I'll stop by your table just as soon as I'm caught up with my orders. How does that sound?"

"Okay, fair enough. Now let me enjoy my coffee and pie."

She flashes a smile and says, "Yes sir."

Thirty-five minutes and three cups of coffee later, Sophia flops down in the chair across from me. "Sorry it took so long. The place is crazy tonight. What did you want to talk to me about?"

I pat the front of my jacket and pull a white envelope out of the breast pocket.

"This is not the ideal place to give you this, but under the circumstances it will have to do." I hand her the envelope. "Mrs. Drummond and I want you to have this."

"What?" she replies with a look of curiosity.

She tears open the envelope and sits back stunned staring at the certified check for forty thousand dollars.

She looks at me and says. "What – what is this? What's this all about? Forty thousand dollars! I can't accept this!"

"Yes, you can. Consider it a down payment on your future and a thank you for bringing such joy and happiness into Valerie's life for so many years. We couldn't have children of our own, so Valerie and I talked about wanting to help you out to find your happiness."

She interrupts me. "But this is a crazy amount of money! How can you afford to give this away?"

"After Valerie's death, I was in no condition to continue working, let alone run a successful business. So, I decided to sell my half of my business to my partner. It made me a fairly wealthy man."

"Seriously, even if you can afford to give me this, it's still too much!"

"Honestly, I wouldn't do this if I couldn't afford to."

Her face lights up. "Are you absolutely sure?"

"Yes."

She jumps out of her chair and gives me a big hug. I can feel her body trembling with excitement. She sits back down, still holding my hand, looks me straight in the eye and says, "Thank you so much, Mr. Drummond. You have no idea how much this means to me. My mother is smiling down at you from heaven right now."

Tears begin to form in her eyes, but I raise my hand to stop her. "No more crying. I want you to be happy and to live a good life."

"And you, Mr. Drummond? What will you do?"

"I'm going to attempt to retire gracefully," I reply, letting out a forced chuckle.

"I promise that I'll put this money to good use."

"I know you will."

I place a ten-dollar bill on the table and stand up. "Will this cover the pie and coffee?"

She takes the money, sticks it into the side pocket of my jacket and says, "I told you this is my treat. Don't argue with me."

I laugh and raise both hands in a sign of surrender. "I wouldn't think of doing that."

She follows me to the exit, hugs me and asks, "When will I see you again?"

"I don't know, dear."

"Promise me you'll come back to see me."

"I'll try."

"Not good enough. Promise me!"

I look to the heavens and think, *Please forgive me for lying.* "Yes, I promise I'll see you again someday. Now, you need to get back to work."

I step out into the chilly night air, look back and wave at Sophia for the final time. *I'm going to miss that girl.*

As I walk across the parking lot toward the highway crossing, I feel stiffness in my legs and I wonder how I'm going to climb up the hill back to my hotel room.

One step at a time, Austin. One step at a time.

As I reach the crosswalk, I notice a young girl trying to thumb a ride north. When she sees me, she waves and says good evening. I watch as another car flies by.

"Where are you headed?" I ask.

"Mendocino."

"What's up there?"

"Work."

"Traveling alone?"

"Yup."

"Aren't you concerned about hitchhiking at night?"

"No more than during the day."

"I guess you're right about that. Anyway, nice meeting you and have a safe trip. Good luck with your new job."

As I begin crossing the highway, she says, "Hey mister. Any chance you could spare a few dollars, so I can get something to eat?"

I turn and walk back toward her. Under the glow of the streetlight, I notice her pretty blue eyes and blond hair. She looks really young, probably not a day over twenty.

"What's your name, young lady?"

"Does it matter?"

I smile. "It does if you want me to give you some money."

"You ain't some kinda weirdo? Are you?"

"That's an odd thing to ask. But to answer your question, no, I'm not."

"Okay. My name is Bonnie."

"Well Bonnie, this may be your lucky day. I just happen to have some spare cash in my pocket that I don't need."

"Really?"

I pull out four fifty-dollar bills and hand them to her.

"Holy crap Mister. Are you sure about this?"

"Consider it my good deed for the day."

"Thanks," she says as she stuffs the bills into her pocket. "Goodnight, Bonnie, and safe travels."

"Cool. Thanks, mister."

Try not to get yourself killed, I think while shaking my head.

Walking up the hill is a bigger struggle than I thought it would be, but I take plenty of rest breaks as I slowly weave my way between the hotel buildings and about fifteen minutes later I'm back inside my room.

I take an Advil, light a fire, pour myself a glass of wine, then remove my shoes and place my aching feet up on the coffee table. The wine, the heat from the fire and the events of the day are catching up to me and I find myself beginning to doze off.

My serenity is interrupted by a pounding noise. It takes me a few seconds to figure out that someone is knocking on the room door.

I stand up too quickly and feel lightheaded for just a moment.

"Hold your horses, I'm coming."

Although groggy, I have the presence of mind to check the peephole before opening the door.

I see a vaguely familiar face staring back at me from the other side of the door and although I only see her face and shoulders, I notice the terrified look on her face; blood is streaming from her nose and there's a tear in her blouse, exposing her shoulder.

"Bonnie?"

"Help me!" she says softly.

"What's wrong?"

"Please help me! I think he's still out here."

"Who's out there?"

"The man who tried to rape me," she says, as her voice breaks and she begins to sob.

"Oh dear God, are you okay?" I release the latch on the room door lock. I hesitate for a split second before opening, and the thought flashes through my mind, *How did she know this is my room?*

The door bursts open, slams into my chest and sends me flying backwards into the near wall. I feel my head strike a solid surface and everything goes dark.

* * *

I'm not sure how long I've been unconscious, but I wake up to find myself sitting on the floor with my back to the wall. My legs are bound with tape, and so are my wrists—behind my back—and another piece of tape is stuck over my mouth. I have a throbbing pain in the back of my head and I see stars when I try to move my neck.

I wince from the pain and a groan is all the sound I can produce.

"Well, look who finally woke up," says the stranger seated at the table to Bonnie, who is sitting on the bed reading a book, looking much cleaner now.

He's not very big, but he's muscular, and his arms and neck are completely covered in tattoos, including crosses on either side below each ear. He's wearing a 2014 Daytona Beach Bike Week t-shirt, worn out jeans and cowboy boots that should have been retired years ago. His shoulder length hair and unkempt beard compliment the hard lines on his face and the scar under his right eye. In fact, he's the spitting image of late-sixties mass murder and cult leader Charles Manson.

Bonnie, on the other hand, looks like your average all-American girl, now that she's cleaned up her face and rinsed out her shirt. She's no raving beauty, but she has a cute face, an upturned nose and soft shiny hair. If I didn't know better, I'd almost say she was sweet. But how sweet can she be hanging around with a dirt bag like this guy at the table?

"You look like shit, Mr. Drummond, or can I call you Austin?" he asks, holding my wallet and staring at my driver's license.

He pulls my debit card out and throws the wallet into the waste basket. "What kinda man travels with no credit cards?"

"How you feeling Mr. Drummond?" Bonnie asks in a sarcastic tone as she flips to the next page in her book.

"Who gives a shit how he feels? I need you to double check through his bag and clothes and see if you can find any more money or credit cards."

"I already did, Clyde. All I found was ten bucks in his jacket pocket."

Bonnie and Clyde! Is this a joke? I think.

Clyde gets up, grabs his jacket from the back of the chair and walks toward the door.

"Well, do it again!" He says.

Bonnie drops her feet over the side of the bed and asks, "Where are you going?"

"I'm gonna walk down to the gas station and buy us some beer, courtesy of our new buddy, Austin."

"Get me some lotto tickets."

"You and them damn lotto tickets. How many times I gotta tell you they're a waste of money?"

Bonnie laughs. "And the beer ain't?"

"Fine. Make sure this guy don't move and when I get back we're gonna have us some fun," he says, grabbing himself between the legs.

"You know I ain't got no more condoms, Clyde."

He bursts out laughing. "That ain't where I was planning on putting it."

She makes a purring sound and says, "Oh, baby, I can hardly wait," but the smile vanishes from her face the minute he closes the door.

She starts rummaging through my bag and the clothes hanging in the closet, but when she doesn't find anything of value, she wanders back to the bed, puts her feet up and goes back to reading her book. I can't help but notice that she's reading one of those sappy Nicholas Sparks novels. She unknowingly begins playing with her hair as she reads and I'm struck by how young and innocent she looks sitting there.

Is she even old enough to drink? I wonder, then pull myself up short. *Why the hell should I care what happens to her? She chose this life, didn't she?*

The more I stare at her, the more I'm reminded of Sophia. I'm starting to convince myself that maybe she doesn't deserve the fate she's been handed. If I have one good deed left in me, I better work fast.

"Misten oo me, I han helm oo ou" I say, hoping to get her attention.

She stares over at me. "What?"

I try to repeat what I said, but it only comes out as a mumble, so I just plead with my eyes.

She walks over and drops to one knee. "I'll loosen the tape over your mouth, if you promise not to scream?"

I nod hard.

She loosens the tape over my mouth. "What do you want?"

"Why are you doing this to me? I gave you money. I helped you!"

"Ain't nothing personal, mister. You're just at the wrong place at the wrong time."

"Well, what are you planning to do with me?"

"I'd rather not say."

"Why don't you just take my car and money and leave?"

"Clyde doesn't like to leave loose ends."

"So, you've done this before?"

She turns her head away and repeats her previous answer. "I'd rather not say."

"If you plan on killing me, you know you'll get caught and spend the rest of your life in prison."

"I ain't the one you got to worry about."

"Even if Clyde is the one who kills me, you'll still be an accessory to murder."

"Well, too late to do anything about that."

"It's never too late. You don't have to do this. I have the financial means to help you get away from this loser. I can set you up for life, give you a second chance."

"Why should I believe you?"

"Because I'm telling you the truth and you have nothing to lose. Untie me and we'll go to the police. I'll vouch for you. I'll tell them that you're just a terrified kid who only did what Clyde wanted because he beat you and threatened to kill you. I'll say I witnessed it myself."

"But that would be a lie."

"I'm not so sure. Is it a lie?"

"I ain't gonna lie about it."

"What? I saw your performance earlier, I know you're a good little actress. And acting is one step away from lying."

"And why would you do this for me?"

"Because you have your whole life ahead of you and don't deserve to die young or spend the rest of your life behind bars."

Her eyes open wide and she slaps me across the face. "Are you threatening me?"

"No, it's not like that..."

She cuts me off in mid-sentence. "You have no idea what you're fucking talking about, mister. I've known guys like you my whole life. My father left when I was three years old and my mother worked herself to death to support us. I've been alone since I was ten, been through the fucking foster care system, where rich family men like you promised me the world—all I had to do was have sex with them and not tell their wives." She gives a bitter laugh.

"I'm sorry you had to go through that, but those men aren't me."

"Oh bullshit—bullshit! If it wasn't for Jesus I'd still be hooking in L.A. He took me out of that shithole and gave me a new life."

"Clyde's real name is Jesus?" I say.

Her face turns red. "I... I didn't say that. I mean Jesus my lord and savior pulled me out of that mess, he used Clyde as his vessel."

"Vessel? Now it's my turn to say 'bullshit', Bonnie... if that's even your real name?"

"Shut the hell up. If you mention one word of this to Clyde, I swear I'll kill you myself." The look on her face tells me she isn't kidding.

I shake my head. "This is going to end badly, Bonnie. I know you don't believe me, but I'm your only chance to save yourself."

"Just because you managed to shut up that starry-eyed girl in the restaurant by offering her money doesn't mean I'm stupid enough to believe that you gave her that check out of the goodness of your heart. How many times did she go down on you to earn that kinda payoff?"

The surprised look on my face must have given away what I was thinking, because she chuckles and says, "Dude, you were so googly-eyed over that girl that you didn't even notice we were sitting at the next table listening to your conversation. Did you?"

I realize that nothing I say is going to change her mind.

"I can't believe I felt sorry for you. You can just burn in hell with your buddy Clyde/Jesus, or whatever the hell his name is."

That earns me another slap across the face, but it's worth it.

She sticks the tape back over my mouth, this time tighter than before. Then she begins removing her clothes in striptease fashion until she's down to her underwear and bra.

As she lowers a strap on her bra with one hand, she squeezes my face tightly with the other and says, "You want to see what your money can't buy, old man?"

I close my eyes and refuse to give her that satisfaction.

She pats my right cheek. "Suit yourself, old man."

I turn away and listen as she walks back to the bed and jumps in.

How could I have been this wrong about her? I guess that's why Val used to kid me about being a sucker for every lost cause.

A few minutes later I hear the door unlock, and Clyde strolls in carrying an open case of beer. He crushes an empty can with his hand, belches and throws it at me.

Bonnie looks at him and says, "I see you started drinking without me?"

"I'm just getting started, baby cakes," he says, dropping the case of beer on the table and unzipping his fly. "Come to Poppa, Baby."

"First, let me see them lotto tickets."

He pulls the tickets out of his back pocket, smiles and turns toward me. "Hey loser, wanna see what a real man looks like? I don't mind if you watch."

Bonnie snatches the tickets from his hand and kneels in front of him. That is about as much as I'm willing to watch, so I turn away.

I hear Clyde laugh. "We got us a pussy here."

Two minutes later, I hear him groan. I smile and think, *Now we know who the real pussy is.*

I hear Clyde zip up and ask Bonnie to fetch him a beer.

"Go easy on that beer, big guy. We got a long drive tonight."

"Goddamn it, Bonnie," Clyde snaps, "don't tell me what to do! I hate it when you tell me what to do!"

"Yes, Clyde."

"Did you find anything in his stuff?"

"Nothing," she replies, and begins scratching her lotto tickets.

Clyde sucks back half his beer. "So, the two hundred bucks he gave you and the ten you found in his jacket was all he had on him?"

"Looks that way."

"So, except for this fucking debit card," he says, holding it up to the light, "he ain't got anything else to offer."

"We ain't gonna be able to use that without a PIN number, Clyde."

"I know that! You think I'm some idiot?"

Staring at him, I think, *Ah! – I'll answer that.*

"No, I was just saying..."

Clyde cuts her off in mid-sentence, "I'm sure Pussy won't mind giving us the PIN number. He won't need it where he's going."

"Up yours," I say through the tape.

"What did you say?" He rips the tape away from my mouth.

"You heard me. Up yours, Jesus."

Bonnie's face turns white.

"How the hell do you know my name?" Clyde hisses.

Bonnie begins stuttering, "I... I... I can explain."

He points at her and says, "Shut up, bitch. I want him to explain." He hits me across the face. "Now tell me how you know my name?"

Bonnie looks like she's about to faint.

"The word is tattooed on both sides of your neck. So, I took a guess. I didn't know that was your real name until you acknowledged it just now."

He smiles and stubs his thumb into my forehead. "Well ain't you a sneaky son of a bitch. Now let's see how brave you are?"

Clyde throws me down on my stomach, grabs the tape wrapped around my wrists and pulls it up toward him.

"Now, I'm gonna ask you for the PIN number, and if you don't give it to me, I'm gonna break one of your fingers. And I'll keep on going like that until you give me the number."

I can feel him bend my right index finger back and pain shoots up my arm.

I stare up at Bonnie and see the terrified look on her face. *Last chance,* I mouth at her. *Help me!*

She shakes her head, and her lips form the words, *I can't. He'll kill me.*

I think, *I'm sorry Valerie. I gave her one last chance. I guess her fate is sealed.*

"Stop!" I scream, and Clyde relieves the pressure on my finger.

"What's the damn pin number?"

"Thirty-three fifty," I say. He slaps the tape back over my mouth. "Jeez, you're a bigger pussy than I thought." Then he bends my finger in the opposite direction until I scream in agony as it snaps with a searing pain.

Clyde laughs, yanks me up by the shoulders and slams me back against the wall. He sees the tears and pats me hard on both cheeks. "You better hope that PIN number works, Pussy, or you're gonna be in a world of hurt."

He turns toward Bonnie and hands her the debit card. "There's an ATM in the gas station. Put your clothes on and go get us some dough."

"Okay, Clyde."

"And get another case of beer."

"I—"

He presses his finger against her lips and she goes silent.

"Think before you speak, bitch."

She nods her head obediently, quickly puts her blouse and jeans back on, then walks out the door.

Twenty minutes later and Bonnie still hasn't returned. Clyde's almost finished the first case of beer and is probably thinking what I'm thinking.

Is she coming back?

Then I hear the door lock open and Bonnie walks in.

"What the hell took so long? Don't tell me the PIN number didn't work?"

"It worked, but you didn't tell me that the ATM in the gas station is busted."

"Shit. How was I supposed to know that?"

"I had to go across to the market and I had to talk the nice security guard into letting me in to use the ATM because they were closing the doors."

"So how much did you get?"

"Five hundred bucks."

"What? That's it?"

"Yup. Looks like Mister Drummond has a limit on how much he can withdraw each day."

If they could see my mouth beneath the duct tape, they'd see me smiling at this one small victory.

Clyde looks over at me and chuckles. "I guess it don't matter. We'll get more money tomorrow. I'm sure Pussy don't mind us keeping his card a few more days."

Bonnie stares around the room, looking at all the empty beer cans scattered across the floor. "You finished the entire case."

The speed at which Clyde's fist strikes Bonnie's face catches me by surprise.

"What did I fucking tell you? Don't fucking tell me what to do! Why can't you just listen and do what I say? You know I don't mean to hurt you, but sometimes you just ask for it."

Bonnie grabs her cheek and catches herself on a sob. "I'm sorry, Clyde," she whispers, and then sits quietly on the bed.

Clyde grabs a couple of beers from the new case and brings one to her.

"Here - have a beer with me, you'll feel better."

She reaches for the beer can, but he pulls it away.

He sees the look of confusion on her face and laughs. "We'll be outta here just after two in the morning, and you're gonna drive. No drinking tonight."

A look of panic crosses her face. "What?"

"You heard me. You're driving, so get some rest."

"But you know I hate driving at night, especially around here."

Clyde takes a swig of beer. "Don't worry, we'll take it slow."

"Why don't you drive?"

He raises his hand to strike her but stops himself. "Just do what I tell you."

"I don't understand."

"I'll be in the back seat watching Pussy."

"What for? He ain't going nowhere?"

"Desperate men do desperate things, and I need to make sure nothing goes wrong."

"But I—"

Clyde clasps his big hand over her mouth before she can continue.

"You need to shut up and do what I say, baby. You're going to drive us to Duncan's Landing and I'm going to take care of Pussy. Then we're gonna go south out of the State. You get it?"

He releases his hand from over her mouth and she says, "When they find his body the cops are gonna come after us."

"I know, but we should be at the Mexican border by then. Once we get across we'll ditch the car and disappear."

A look of relief crosses her face. "You promise?"

"Yes. I promise," he replies, taking another big gulp of beer.

Bonnie jumps up and hugs him, then turns toward me and sticks her tongue out, as if to say, I told you so.

Clyde grabs her butt cheeks and says. "Set the alarm clock for two and get some rest. We got a long ride ahead of us."

She does what she's told and within minutes, I hear her breathing deeply as she sleeps.

Clyde sits in the chair, opens another beer and stares at me. Every once in a while I notice his eyelids shut, and then pop back open again. Around midnight he stands up, belches, and says, "I gotta take a piss."

I close my eyes and I find myself safe and warm, in Valerie's arms. I remember the first time I laid eyes on her, the first time we made love, and the day I told her that I loved her.

I recall the love I felt on my wedding day and how every night at bedtime she'd tell me how much she loved me. I was the luckiest man in the world.

You have no idea how much I miss you, Sweetheart.

My beautiful memories are interrupted by the sound of a flushing toilet and the creaking hinges of the bathroom door.

As Clyde walks past me, he smirks. "Won't be much longer, Pussy. This might be a good time to start saying your prayers."

* * *

The alarm clock rings at 2:00 AM and I watch as Bonnie reaches for the off button. Clyde has finished all the beer and fallen asleep in the chair. I was in and out during that time, dreaming about Valerie and fighting the throbbing pain from my broken finger.

Clyde opens his eyes, yawns, stretches and scratches his crotch.

"God, I got a splitting headache."

Bonnie chimes in, "I told you not to…"

Clyde gives her a look that says, If you finish that sentence I'll slug you again.

She nods in understanding.

"All right, baby, pick up all his shit and throw it in the car. Let me know if all's clear before I carry him down."

"Sure, Clyde."

Bonnie takes my clothes from the drawer, my jacket from the closet, and the toiletries off the bathroom counter. She stuffs it all in my overnight bag and takes it downstairs.

She returns right away and gives Clyde a nervous looking thumbs up. Clyde yanks me up from the ground, swings me over his shoulder like a sack of potatoes, and takes me down the stairs to the car. He opens the passenger front door, flips forward the passenger seat, and shoves me into the back seat behind the driver. Then he farts and sits down next to me, the sour smell of his body filling my nostrils.

I'm overcome with sadness when I realize that the silver vial with Valerie's ashes is still in my jacket pocket and I won't be taking her with me.

I close my eyes and feel the lump in my throat. *Sorry Val. It wasn't supposed to end this way.*

Clyde puts his arm around me, and I have to fight down my gag reflex. "Have you ever been to Duncan's Landing? I hear it's beautiful at this time of the morning. The sound of the waves crashing against the rocks is so loud that you can barely hear yourself think, let alone scream." He laughs and his breath stinks of beer.

Bonnie gets behind the wheel, straps on her seatbelt and says, "I need some fresh air." She turns the ignition key to open the windows and the sunroof, then starts the engine.

Suddenly the CD player blasts the sound of Chris de Burgh, singing the song, *Flying Home.*

"And we are flying home,
I feel the freedom in my soul,
Flying home at last."

Everyone is stunned for a moment. Then Clyde screams, "Turn that damn thing off!"

How appropriate, I think, as Bonnie ejects the CD and tosses it out the window.

"Ok, enough of this shit," Clyde says. "I need you to drive real slow until we get to the highway, then turn right and head north."

"I know where I'm going, Clyde. Don't make me more nervous than I already am."

Clyde chuckles, slaps me on the shoulder and says, "Pussy here says you'll be just fine. Right, Buddy?"

I stare at him and think, *Don't count on it, asshole.*

Bonnie coasts carefully down to Highway 1 and turns right. Under the bright moonlight I take one last look at The Tides Wharf Restaurant and Bodega Bay. My mind shifts to thoughts of Sophia and I smile, knowing she'll be all right. *Goodbye, dear friend.*

Bonnie drives the car slowly through town, until she reaches the looping right hand turn. I feel the cool breeze through the open windows and notice that all the houses in Bodega Bay are dark; everyone is safe and sound sleeping in their beds. Somehow that thought gives me comfort.

As we pass Pelican Plaza Grocery & Deli and Bodega Bay Grange Hall, the highway begins a long decline down to a hairpin turn, before continuing back up the hill.

I feel the car speed up and I hear Bonnie pump the brakes.

Clyde leans forward and says, "Slow down."

Bonnie's voice is sounding panicked. "I'm trying to, but the brakes feel funny!"

Clyde buckles his seatbelt and says, "What the hell are you talking about? Slow the hell down! Now!"

The car continues to accelerate, and Bonnie begins screaming. "I can't stop, there's something wrong!"

"Pull the fucking handbrake, you idiot!"

She does as she's told, but the car continues to accelerate.

Clyde turns to me, rips the tape off my mouth and sticks a gun to the side of my head. "What the hell did you do to the brakes?"

I look straight ahead and begin praying out loud.

"Our Father, who art in heaven, hallowed be thy name. Thy kingdom come, thy will be done, on earth…"

"Shut up, shut up! What did you do to the damn brakes?"

"… as it is in heaven. Give us this day our…"

I feel the car picking up speed. We are approaching the hairpin turn, and the car begins sliding sideways onto the gravel shoulder as Bonnie cranks the steering wheel in a desperate attempt to keep it on the road. For just a moment our eyes meet in the rearview mirror, and I notice the sheer terror in her face.

I tried to warn you, sweetheart. Now it's too late.

Clyde turns toward Bonnie, screaming at her to stay on the road. The car is spinning out of control, and the force slams my body into Clyde's arm. I hear the gun go off. Bonnie's head jerks sideways with the impact of the bullet to the back of her head, and she slumps forward against the steering wheel.

Time seems to stand still as I feel the car begin to flip sideways over the edge of the embankment toward the rocks below. Clyde desperately fumbles with his seatbelt, but it's too late.

As the car goes airborne, I catch a glimpse of the stars through the sunroof and think, *Meet me at the Pearly Gates Val. I'm flying home.*

I feel my body exiting the vehicle and my world goes dark.

* * *

I see a bright light flash over my eyelids. It swings back and forth across my line of sight, but I can't seem to open my eyes. I hear an odd sound, but I don't immediately recognize it. The sound continues until it's accompanied by a voice.

It's calling my name, "Wake up, Mr. Drummond. Austin! Time to wake up."

Suddenly I recognize the noise—it's the sound of fingers snapping. My eyes pop open, just as the word "God" inadvertently leaves my lips.

I stare at an elderly man, dressed in white. He's wearing glasses and is sporting a gray beard and a receding hairline.

He smiles down at me. "Welcome back, Mr. Drummond."

He picks up my right arm, turns it over and places his thumb against the inside of my wrist.

Confused, I ask, "Are you God?"

He laughs. "Heck no!"

"What are you doing?"

"Monitoring your heart rate."

"Am I dead?"

"Dead, no; confused, yes," he replies with another laugh.

"Who are you, and where am I?"

"My name is Dr. Clueski, and you're in Sebastopol General Hospital."

"What am I doing here?"

"You don't remember?"

I shake my head and pain shoots down the back of my spine.

"Please try not to move, Mr. Drummond."

"Am I going to be okay?" I ask with difficulty.

"Yes, but you'll be here for a while. The accident left you with a broken leg, fractured ribs, a nasty bump on the back of your head, and lots of cuts and bruises."

He sees the look of confusion.

"You were in an automobile accident, suffered a concussion and were in a coma for three days. You're lucky to be alive, Mr. Drummond. It was a miracle that you were thrown from the vehicle because that's what probably saved your life."

I wince from the pain and think, *At this moment, I don't feel all that lucky.*

"Try to relax, I'll send the nurse in and she'll give you something to make you comfortable."

"Dr. Clueski, what happened to the other people in the car?"

"Ah, so you're beginning to remember some details about what happened. Don't worry, it will all come back to you in due time."

"You didn't answer my question."

"That's because I'm not at liberty to say. I'm certain that the police will fill in the missing pieces."

"The police?"

"Yes. Once I inform them that you're out of the coma, they'll be around to ask you some questions. In the meantime, please get some rest."

I nod my head and immediately regret it, then just say, "Great."

"For someone who's lucky to be alive, you sure don't seem grateful, Mr. Drummond."

That's because I'm not!

I close my eyes and feel myself slipping off to sleep when someone gently touches me on the shoulder.

"Mr. Drummond, the Doctor wants you to take these, please open your mouth." A nurse places two pills on my tongue and puts a cup against my lips so I can wash them down with cold water. "They'll help you with the pain."

As I thank her, I see Dr. Clueski standing at the edge of the bed tapping on the screen of his tablet.

The nurse sticks something in my ear. "By the way, my name is Nurse Ella." She pulls the device back out of my ear, looks at it and mutters a number. Then she asks, "How are you feeling, Mr. Drummond? You gave us quite a scare, but I'm glad to see that you're awake and talking."

I close my eyes. "My body feels like it's just gone through twelve rounds of a heavy weight boxing match," I say, and my voice feels like sandpaper.

"Are you a boxer?"

"No, but I imagine that this is what going twelve rounds would feel like."

"Well, at least you haven't lost your sense of humor, Mr. Drummond," she says.

"Yeah, I guess."

She adjusts my pillow and says, "It's really important that you try to remain positive, Mr. Drummond. Studies show that patients with positive attitudes heal faster."

Really, and what does it say about patients who'd rather be dead? I think, then open my eyes and whisper, "Thank you, Nurse."

Dr. Clueski taps his fingers on the bed railing and says, "Get some rest, Mr. Drummond. Everything will be clearer in a day or two. I'll drop by later to look in on you."

"Sure, doc."

As they're turning away, Nurse Ella puts her hand on Dr. Clueski's arm.

"There's a young lady here who's been waiting for him to wake up. Can she come in to see him?"

Dr. Clueski pauses, then replies, "Okay, but only for a few minutes. Hopefully, she'll help him out of his funk."

"Yes, Doctor."

A moment later I hear Nurse Ella say, "Mr. Drummond, there's someone here to see you."

I keep my eyes closed. "I don't know if I want any company right now."

"She's been very concerned about you and has been waiting three days to see you. Are you sure you can't give her a minute to say hello?"

"Hello Mr. Drummond. It's me, Sophia."

"Sophia," I say as I open my eyes.

"I'm sorry to bother you. I can come back some other time," she says, turning to leave.

"No. No. Please don't go."

She turns around slowly, and I notice the swollen bags under her eyes.

"I'm sorry if I upset you, Sophia," I say, stretching my good arm toward her, "I'm just a little confused right now. Please forgive me."

She takes my hand. "There's nothing to forgive, Mr. Drummond. I'm just so glad you're okay. You really had me worried; I didn't think you were going to make it."

I give her a weak smile and think, *Jesus, I even failed at suicide.*

"I have something for you," she says with an excited tone in her voice.

"You do?" I feel flat, unable to bring up any emotion.

She smiles at me, reaches into her purse, takes something out and places it in the palm of my hand. It takes a second to register, but then I recognize it: the silver vial containing Valerie's ashes.

"Oh my God. Oh my God – I thought I lost this forever. How? Where did you find this?"

I feel moisture building in the corner of my eyes.

"The cleaning person found it in the restaurant the morning after your visit. It was under the table where you were sitting, and when I saw the name *'Drummond'* inscribed on it, I knew it was yours."

Now warm tears are falling, as I clutch the vial tightly in my hand.

"I tried to get it back to you that morning, Mr. Drummond, but the hotel staff told me you'd left during the night. When I heard the news about the accident, I came here as soon as I could."

"Thank you, Sophia. You have no idea how much this means to me."

"You're welcome, Mr. Drummond. So, it's important?" she asks with an inquisitive look.

"Yes. It's my Valerie's ashes. When I had her body cremated, I couldn't stand the thought of tossing all her ashes into the Pacific and losing her forever, so I had some of her ashes placed in this little vial. I know it sounds silly, but it was very comforting at the time."

"I don't think it's silly at all. I think it shows just how much you love and miss her."

"Yeah. I miss her so much that I've misplaced this vial twice since I've been here. If she's looking down on me, she probably thinks I'm awful."

"I doubt that Mr. Drummond. In fact, I think that she's sending you a sign."

I roll my eyes. "A sign? And what sign might that be?"

"Well, don't you think it's odd that each time you lost the vial, someone returned it safely to you?"

"Sophia, I'm not so sure that's a sign as much as it's just sheer luck."

"I think you're wrong. I think that she's trying to tell you that no matter what happens, she'll always be with you."

I smile and say, "That's a beautiful thought, but I don't know if I believe in signs. Not anymore."

She clears her throat and says, "There's something else I need to tell you, but I don't want you to think I'm crazy and I don't want to add to your confusion."

"Don't worry; I won't think you're crazy. As for adding to my confusion, I don't think I can be any more confused than I already am. So, what is it, Sophia? What is it you need to tell me?"

She hesitates as she runs her fingers along the edge of the bed spread.

"While I was sitting in the waiting room hoping and praying that you would wake from your coma, I had a vision."

"A vision?" *Maybe I spoke too soon about thinking she's not crazy.*

She looks up at me and I can see that she's unsure whether to tell me or keep it to herself.

"After everything I've been through, I don't think you need to worry about upsetting me. Please tell me about the dream." *Let's get this over with, I'm tired.*

"Mrs. Drummond was in the dream."

You have my attention. "What is it, Sophia? Whatever it is, it can't be that bad."

"It's not bad at all, it's just confusing."

"Confusing?"

"She told me to give you a message."

"Really!" *This should be good.*

"Yes. She said to tell you that she heard you and that she'll be waiting at the Pearly Gates when the time is right."

"What did you say?" I reply abruptly.

I see the painful look on Sophia's face. "Now I've upset you. That's what I didn't want to happen."

"No, no, you haven't upset me," I reply as tears begin streaming.

"But you're crying."

"Yes, but they're tears of joy."

A bewildered look crosses her face. "Tears of joy?"

I realize that I can't ignore it any longer.

"Yes. It's a sign."

She looks confused. "But you just told me you don't believe in signs."

I can't contain myself. "It means that someday I'll be with my Valerie again!"

She sees the genuine excitement in my eyes, and smiles. "So, it's a good sign."

"Yes, it's a wonderful, life-altering sign. Something I've been waiting for since the day Valerie passed away. I can't thank you enough for telling me. Val always said you were an angel, and now I know what she meant."

She squeezes my hand and smiles at me. "I guess the only thing left to say is… Amen."

"Amen indeed!" It comes out as a shout, as I pull her towards me and hug her to my shoulder.

For the first time since Valerie's death, my heart is filled with joy—a joy that I know will last me the rest of my mortal life.

Things We Can't Control

I sit quietly on a park bench overlooking the gardens at Happy Haven Retirement home.

I glance at my watch and notice that my buddy Jonesy is twenty minutes late. This is the fifth time this week that he has kept me waiting and with each passing day, he seems to be arriving later and later.

I rest my cane against the bench and grab the water bottle from my coat pocket. I take a sip of water to quench my dry throat then return it to my pocket.

Where the hell are you, Jonesy? I think. *You know I hate it when you keep me waiting?*

Jonesy and I met six years ago, when my daughter Heather and son-in-law Barry admitted me to Happy Haven against my will. I thought I was doing just fine living at home by myself, but my daughter disagreed.

So what, if every once in awhile, I wondered off in the neighborhood and forgot how to get back home, everyone knew me, so there was always someone who would escort me back to the house. No big deal, right! I thought.

Unfortunately, I couldn't convince Heather and Barry that I'd be fine living alone.

I think I would have been okay moving in with my daughter, son-in-law and the grand kids, but unfortunately their home is too small to accommodate another person. So for my own good, they forced me into moving into this managed care facility.

Don't get me wrong. Happy Haven is a first-class facility, so I don't hate the place, but it's not home, it will never be my home. Heather and the kids come to visit once a week, but if it wasn't for Jonesy living here, I'd go stir crazy in this place.

While deep in my own thoughts, I fail to notice that someone is standing next to me, until I hear them clear their throat.

"Talking to yourself again, are you?" Jonesy says letting out a laugh.

"You're late, Mr. Jones. That's the fifth time this week, but who's counting."

He snickers. "Obviously, you are!"

"You find that amusing?"

"No, but I must say that you've got a pretty good memory for a guy who wonders off and forgets his way home."

"Ha, Ha. You're too funny, Jonesy."

He smiles. "Thank you, Joseph. I'll take that as a compliment."

As Jonesy sits down on the bench, I hear his knees crack. He lets out an old person groan, as he adjusts his rear end on the bench. He places his cup of coffee down on the bench between us, and farts.

"Geez, Jonesy. Are you kidding me?"

He shrugs his shoulders. "Sorry, it couldn't be helped. It was beyond my control."

"Well I hope you're wearing your man diapers today." I blurt out just before I begin my coughing fit.

I see the smirk on his lips. "Oh, Ha, Ha. Ha! Now who's the damn comedian?"

Jonesy pats me on the back a couple of times, in an attempt to help me control my fit of coughing and laughing. It takes about thirty seconds, but I finally catch my breath and manage to regain control.

"It sure sucks getting old. Doesn't it, Joseph?"

I smile and nod without saying a word, then pull out a tissue and blow my nose. "So where were you? Are you doing this to piss me off?"

"Sorry, I slept in again."

"You slept in again!"

"Yup! It seems to be getting harder and harder for me to get my ass out of bed every day."

"That's because you're an old fart."

"Oh, look who's talking... *Mister* six months younger than me."

We both laugh, but I notice by the look on Jonesy's face that something is bothering him.

"I saw that look, my friend. What's wrong? Talk to me."

"What do you mean?" He says trying to hide the flash of fear I noticed in his eyes.

"Don't tell me, you had another dream?"

Jonesy rubs his chin before answering. "I'd say more like a nightmare ... a reoccurring nightmare."

"Same dream over and over again?"

"Not exactly the same, but close. This time I couldn't figure out how to get back home. When I woke up, I was bawling like a baby."

I try to make light of it, "I know the feeling, my friend, but it's just a dream."

"But it seems so darn real. It always begins with me driving to work."

"Driving to work? You've been retired for twenty years!"

He ignores my comment and continues his story.

"The first time it happened, my office had been moved without me knowing it. I searched all day to find it, but no one in the building could help me, because everyone at work was someone I'd never met before. The next night, I dreamt that I found my office, but my desk and all my things were gone. The following night my name plate was missing from my office door. When I asked my Supervisor where it went, he had no idea who I was and had me escorted out of the building by security. The next night I dreamt I was leaving work, but I couldn't remember where I parked my car. People tried to help me locate it, but I couldn't remember the make and model. I thought I was having a stroke or something. I woke up in a cold sweat."

I smile and attempt to blow it off. "I'm sure there's a rational explanation. No need to freak out Jonesy. It's just a dream. The good news is that you wake up every day and everything is fine."

"Rational explanation?"

"Yeah. What would Sigmund Freud say?"

"This isn't funny Joseph. It's really beginning to freak me out."

"I'm sure it isn't funny when it's happening, but you really have to put things into perspective."

"What perspective? The fact, that I'm losing my mind!"

"Who said anything about you losing your mind? It's a dream; don't make more of it than it is. If you really feel this terrified, maybe you should consider talking to one of the Happy Haven counselors."

He shakes his head and once again acts as if he didn't hear a word I said.

"I feel lost Joseph. I feel like I'm losing my place in the world. It's as if I don't belong here anymore."

I can see by the look on his face that this is really weighing heavily on my friend and I'm not sure how to help the poor guy. *Maybe, if I share one of my dreams with him, it will make him realize that his world is not coming to an end and that he's not the only one who has crazy dreams.*

"Wait until I tell you about the dream I had last night? Talk about a bloody nightmare."

"Let me guess? You were having sex with a playboy bunny when your wife walks in!"

"No, but that actually did happen." I reply and burst into laughter.

Jonesy smiles, but I can see that his heart is not in it. This is more serious than I thought.

"Anyway, I dreamed that I bought a scratch off lottery ticket and won 3 million dollars."

"*That's,* what you call a nightmare?"

"No," I reply, "the nightmare comes when I accidentally run the winning ticket through a paper shredder."

"How in the world did you do that?" He asks with a look of disbelief.

I shrug my shoulders. "How should I know? It's a stupid dream. It's not like I have any control over it!"

He rolls his eyes. "So, what happened?"

"As I recall, I placed the winning ticket on my kitchen table, right next to a stack of documents I was getting ready to shred. Somehow the ticket fell in with the documents and before I could stop myself, I fed it through the shredder."

"You what?"

"I spent the next day trying to tape the tiny, shredded pieces of the ticket back together, only to have the guy at the Lottery Office tell me that the ticket in its present form could not be redeemed."

"That's unbelievable!"

"The unbelievable part is that I've never owned a paper shredder."

I see a smile form on his lips. "Oh crap! That is a nightmare."

"I still get chills when I think about it."

"How did the dream end?"

I smile, shrug my shoulders and throw my hands in the air. "I have no idea… that's when I woke up screaming like a banshee."

He looks at me and this time laughs out loud. "That was you I heard screaming this morning?"

"Not my proudest moment, my friend."

He throws me a genuine smile. "Thanks Joseph. You always knew how to say the right thing. Thank you for always making me smile. I really miss you."

His words send a chill down my spine. "What do you mean by that, Jonesy?"

"I mean it's time for you to come upstairs, breakfast is ready."

I feel my eye lids pop open and find myself staring into the beautiful face of my nurse, my guardian angel, Marabel.

I see the sympathetic look, as she places her arm under mine and begins to lift me up off the bench.

"You're talking to Mr. Jones again, aren't you?"

I look around in confusion. "Yes. Where is he? He was right here!" I say pointing at the bench.

Marabel puts her arm around me and softly rubs my back. "We both know that Mr. Jones is no longer with us."

"He can't leave." I say with the sound of desperation ringing in my voice.

"Honey, I don't think Mr. Jones wanted to leave you, but it wasn't up to him."

I feel tears forming. "But, but... we had a bet."

"A bet?"

"He owes me money!"

She fastens the top button on my shirt. "What bet was that Sweetie?"

"We bet on who would go first!"

She replies in a soft, soothing voice, "and you lost?"

I let out a cry and begin to sob. "It wasn't supposed to happen this way! I was supposed to go first!"

"Honey, I've lived long enough to know, that there are two things in this world you can't control. What you dream about and who gets to go first."

I wipe the tears, as she hands me my cane. I lean against her wing, as she guides me down the pathway.

Marabel rubs my shoulder as we continue walking. "Come on Sweetie, your breakfast is getting cold and I'm pretty sure that Mr. Jones has saved you a good seat at the table."

Remorse

It takes several seconds for my eyes to adjust as I enter the seedy, dimly lit pub. My senses are immediately assaulted by the smell of stale beer, mold, and vomit. A handful of patrons are scattered about the room, packed in booths, too busy nursing their drinks to notice me as I make my way toward the bar.

A man, presumably the bartender, stands at one end of the counter, reading a racing form. I can't help but notice the toothpick dangling between his teeth. He raises his head. "What can I get you, buddy?"

"A Bud on tap."

"One Bud draft coming up," he replies, giving me a cheesy, yellow-toothed smile.

I glance down at the countertop and notice that it's filthy. I find myself hoping that the glasses are cleaned more frequently than the countertop, but as the bartender slides the beer across the counter toward me, I see the lipstick stain on the rim and know that my hopes are for naught.

I turn to thank him, but he's already back to reading his form.

I can't bring myself to drink the beer, so I set it aside and pull back my sleeve to check my watch. It's two-twenty in the afternoon. The man on the telephone told me to meet him here at two-thirty. I'm ten minutes early.

A part of me still can't believe that I'm really doing this.

But after months of tears, heartache, and anger, I've come to the conclusion that my ex-wife has to die.

I wasted ten years of my life on a woman who swore up and down that she loved me and would never be unfaithful, only to discover it was all a damn lie. Ten years of loving this woman with all my heart, even after we discovered that she couldn't bear me any children.

I treated Sara like a goddamn princess. I never asked her to work, and I never denied her anything she wanted. In return, the ingrate cheated on me.

Upset by the thought, I carelessly grab my beer and take a large mouthful, before remembering the filthy glass. Realizing what I've done, I consider spitting it out on the floor, but instead I choke it down and pound my fist on the bar, hoping I don't get sick from someone else's germs.

The bartender looks up. "Everything alright, buddy?"

"I'll live," I reply while wiping my mouth.

He smirks, mumbles something under his breath and goes back to reading.

Even though I'd suspected Sara was cheating on me, a part of me hadn't wanted to acknowledge the truth. I'd convinced myself that even if she was running around behind my back, I was okay with that, as long as she didn't leave me. Thinking about it now, it seems like an idiotic way of handling the situation.

I'm not a wealthy man, but I do own a successful import-export business, which requires much of my attention including working long hours and traveling a lot. Sara knew all this when she married me, and during the early years of marriage, she would jump at the opportunity to travel around the world and accompany me on my business ventures. But in the past few years she rarely traveled with me, preferring to stay home and take care of the house—at least that's what she led me to believe. Even though I was disappointed in her decision, I respected her wishes.

In hindsight, I was an idiot not to have paid more attention to the little things that had changed in our relationship.

We used to love spending every waking moment together, enjoying each other's company. Simple things like going out for dinner, catching a movie, taking long walks, and stopping for coffee made us happy. When we made love, it was sensual and passionate. Even if we did it every day, we still couldn't get enough of each other.

Just thinking about it makes me miss what we once had.

I suppose we allowed ourselves to drift apart. I paid little attention to my marriage and far too much to my business. When we did talk it was run-of-the-mill and shallow. There were days we hardly saw or spoke to each other and neither one of us made any effort to change the situation. We still made love every once in a while, but the closeness and intimacy were gone. Unlike the early years, there was no passion, and we rarely spoke before or after sex. We were going through the motions and neither one of us seemed to be enjoying it.

I was disappointed with what had become of our relationship, but I thought it was just a phase that married couples go through. Sure, we were in a rut, but we were young and over time the situation would fix itself. Looking back, it sounds so stupidly naive.

About a year ago while I was on business in Dubai, I received an anonymous voice mail, a call I later found out had been made from a hotel phone somewhere near the airport.

I didn't recognize the voice, but it was definitely a man speaking.

"Hello, Mr. Deputer. You probably wouldn't remember me, but I've met you and Mrs. Deputer a few times at various business functions. I'd rather not identify myself because I don't feel comfortable leaving this message. I'm not in the habit of interfering in people's personal lives, but you seem like a decent fellow and I hate seeing good people made to look like fools.

Anyway, there's no good way to tell you this, so I'll just come out and say it.

Last night, I saw your wife with a strange man at a restaurant I frequent often. By strange, I don't mean that he was odd, but that he wasn't you.

Anyway, it isn't the first time I've seen them together. I could be wrong, but their body language and some of the conversation I overheard suggests that they might be more than just friends.

As I said, I'm not one to get involved in other people's lives, but I've recently gone through the same sort of thing with my relationship, and I hate seeing it happen to other people. I sincerely hope I'm wrong about this, but I thought you should know.

Anyway, do what you will with this."

At first, I thought the message was preposterous—Sara would never cheat on me. But once the seed of suspicion had been planted, the allegation was always in the back of my mind. I probably should have confronted my wife with the accusation, but I didn't want to look like a jealous fool accepting the word of a stranger. I should have dropped the whole thing, but my suspicious nature got the better of me and I had to know the truth.

The following week while away on business, I contacted a private investigator and asked him to follow my wife. My hope was that the accusation was complete nonsense and could be laid to rest without Sara ever knowing I had her followed, but to my disappointment, the investigator discovered that everything the stranger had inferred was indeed true.

The most unsettling part of the whole sordid mess was that the man she'd been seeing was in fact a good friend of mine. Morris and I had known each other since high school; I would never have expected this from him.

I'm not sure how long the affair had gone on, but when I finally confronted Sara, she didn't deny it. She looked me straight in the face and told me she was sorry it had happened the way it did. She meant to tell me sooner, but no time seemed to be a good time.

I was crushed by her admission, but I was even more devastated when she informed me that she loved Morris and wanted out of our marriage.

Like a fool, I begged her not to leave me. I promised her I'd cut back on my business trips and we'd spend more time together. I swore that I would try to do everything in my power to make things right by her.

Her response was like a dagger through my heart.

"I'm sorry, Bradley, but there's nothing you can say or do to make things right again. You're a good man, but I don't love you anymore. The feelings I once had for you are gone and it's not something that I can simply turn on or off."

"Did you have sex with him?" I asked.

Her blushing face revealed the truth even though she refused to answer.

"For God's sake, how is this possible? Are you sure that you actually love him?"

"Yes. I love him."

"What about us? What about me? Don't you know how much I love you?

"You claim that you love me, Bradley, but everything you've said and done over the last few years hasn't made me feel either happy or loved. I know that you love your business and I know you love to travel, but I don't feel your love for me."

"That's nonsense. You know that I love you. I've always loved you."

"Love is more than words. Just saying it doesn't make it so. We've been drifting apart for years and neither one of us has cared enough to do anything about it."

"So, it's my fault?"

"It's never just one person's fault. You used to be such a wonderful listener, Bradley, but now you only hear what you want to hear."

"I don't want you to leave, Sara."

"I've fallen in love with someone else and I can't pretend it isn't true. If I don't leave now, who knows how many more years we'll spend in this make-believe relationship."

"The only one pretending is you."

She shook her head, gave me a sympathetic look, and said, "I'm sorry, I don't mean to hurt you, but I have to go. Take care of yourself, Bradley."

Just like that, it was over. Ten years of marriage tossed out the window. The next day she packed just a few suitcases with her clothes and personal possessions.

I'd be fine, she said, and I deserved better than to live with someone who no longer loved me.

What about me? I thought. *What about the fact that I still love you and I want us to stay together?*

I begged her one last time not to go, but she kissed me on the cheek, said goodbye, and walked out the door.

The pain of losing her and the self-doubt that came from blaming myself for everything that had gone wrong left me with an emptiness that I'd never felt before.

I honestly believed that if I'd paid more attention to her needs this would never have happened. The thought tortured me for weeks.

But when the divorce papers finally arrived, I was stunned to discover that Sara and her attorney were requesting a settlement worth half of all I owned.

A settlement? I thought. *It'll be a cold day in hell before I give her one stinking penny.*

I couldn't believe the nerve of her, asking for half the value of my estate, especially after she admitted to cheating on me and leaving of her own free will.

The serving of the divorce papers did something to me that weeks of introspection failed to do. It made me realize that it wasn't my fault. Sara knew exactly what she was doing and nothing I could have done would have changed the course of our marriage.

My feelings of guilt, pain and remorse were replaced by feelings of outrage and hatred towards both of them. I contemplated taking my revenge out on Morris, making him disappear, but I wasn't so sure that he was the one to blame. Sara has always been a good manipulator; she knows how to get exactly what she wants. That poor sap probably never stood a chance.

After all the anguish she put me through, now she thinks she is entitled to half of everything I own. I was feeling pretty confident that once my attorney showed the judge the photographs of my wife's affair, she'd get a big fat nothing.

Unfortunately, it didn't take long to receive the frustrating news from my attorney. Sara hadn't been as dumb as I thought. She'd had me followed on several of my overseas business trips and managed to obtain photographs of my own sexual exploits.

I couldn't believe she'd had me followed. I tried explaining to my attorney that the only reason I had those sexual encounters was because of her. She was the one to blame. If she hadn't stayed home instead of accompanying me like a good wife should, I wouldn't have needed to look elsewhere to satisfy my sexual desires.

"But no, she was too fucking busy at home, banging my friend," I say out loud.

The bartender looks over at me, laughs and says, "Hey buddy, keep it down. Nobody here gives a shit about your personal problems."

I hear a few snickers from across the room as he slides another beer across the counter and tells me it's on the house.

I'm about to tell him to shove it, when I feel someone tap me on the shoulder.

"Mr. Deputer?"

I snap my head around. "What?"

The man looks at me and says, "My name is Dmitri. You called for me."

It takes a second to realize who the man is. Then he crooks his index finger and says, "Follow me to booth."

Dmitri looks nothing like what I expect a killer to look like. He's short, chubby, and bald with a surprisingly ordinary-looking face. I've never met a killer before, but I was expecting a muscular thug with scars on his face or tattoos on his neck. Dmitri plops his ass down in the corner booth and orders a shot of whiskey. I carry my beer over and slide into the seat across from him.

The bartender delivers the shot of whiskey and I watch him wander back to the bar.

Dmitri sips his drink. "You look disappointed Mr. Deputer."

"You're not what I expected."

"Ah," he says while running his finger around the rim of his glass. "You expect big man vith gun in pants, like John Vayne."

He smiles and I notice two teeth missing.

"Sorry, but you don't look like a killer. Do you mind me asking, how many people have you, uh, done away with?"

"Enough," he replies. "Did you bring money?"

"Yes. As we agreed, half now and half when the job is done."

"*Da.*" He takes another sip of his whiskey.

"How will I know when the job is done?"

"I bring you *kartinki*—how you say, pictures. Do you have *kartinki* and address of the person you vant I kill?"

I swallow hard, then pull a folder containing a recent photograph of Sara out of my jacket pocket and place it on the table. Dmitri picks up the folder, looks inside without removing the photograph and says, "Pretty voman, your vife. Are you sure you vant I do this? Once done, no can take back."

I nod, but a part of me can't believe I'm really asking him to do this.

"It has to look like a break-in... a robbery gone bad. Can you do that?" I ask, trying to reassure myself.

"No worry. I make look like robbery gone, how you say? Bad."

I sit nervously running my fingers through my hair as he finishes his drink and orders another.

"Give me *den'gi* under table."

"What?"

He stares at the confused look on my face.

"American dollars! Give under table."

I slip the bulky envelope under the table and watch it disappear into his vest pocket.

He extends his meaty hand and says, "Ve have deal."

I extend my hand and ask him when he thinks the job will be complete.

"Vill be done, vhen done."

"What does that mean?"

"Vill do vhen time is right."

"Soon, I hope? I don't want this stretched out any longer than it needs to be."

He shows the gap in his teeth in a wolfish grin. "Don't vorry. It vill be soon. Ve meet here in two veeks. You bring rest of *den'gi*."

I feel myself nodding like an idiot. *This is what happens when you hire someone sight unseen over the internet*, I think as I watch him get up and push his way out through the doors.

A few minutes later, I step up to the bar to settle my tab, only to discover that Dmitri stiffed me for his two drinks on top of the money I already gave him. I hope this guy is worth it.

Stepping outside, I'm struck by the realization that I just handed someone money to kill my ex-wife. A queasy feeling rolls around in my stomach, and I rush around the corner, heaving, to empty the contents of my stomach into the alleyway.

On the subway ride back to my house, I sit staring at my reflection in the window. I've always wondered what the face of a murderer looks like. I never imagined it would look like mine.

My mind wanders back to the weeks right after the divorce papers were filed. The economy and the stock market had tanked and my business had fallen on hard times. I needed every cent I could get my hands on just to keep my business afloat. Knowing that half of what I had left would probably end up in the hands of my ex and her lover made it all seem pointless, but I dragged on nonetheless. I couldn't think of what else to do. The only thing that dulled my misery was alcohol, lots of alcohol.

Then came the night that set the wheels in motion leading to today's meeting with Dmitri.

It was a Friday evening and I was sitting at the bar in the Princeton Hotel, where I'd spent most evenings lately, staring out the window at the rush hour traffic, when I spotted them. Sara and Morris, walking into the restaurant across the street. The host seated them at a table by the window—a table I knew well. It used to be *our* favorite table. They couldn't see me but I could see them. They looked truly happy and every smile, every time she touched his hand, was like a jab to my heart. I hadn't seen Sara in weeks, but she looked absolutely radiant in the red dress I'd bought her on our last trip to Spain.

I'd almost forgotten how beautiful she was and how much I really missed her.

And then Morris, my former friend, leaned across to Sara, *my wife*, and kissed her. A kiss that grew more and more passionate. I stood paralyzed, staring, as my gut twisted in hate. She reached for his hand, and I could not tear my eyes away from her face. Her mouth shaped the words "I love you." And that was when I wanted to reach across the street and strangle her.

In that moment I knew that I couldn't sit by and watch my wife and her lover live a life of luxury at my expense. There was no fucking way I could live with that. But as long as she was alive, she would find a way to get at my money. So that night as I lay in bed staring at the ceiling I swore that she would have to die.

* * *

Dmitri has gotten to the bar before me for our second meeting. He is already sitting at a booth, sucking back another whiskey.

The last couple of weeks, I've done everything I could to keep myself occupied and in the public eye. I know I'll need a good alibi for whenever this thing went down, so I had dinner with friends, visited relatives I haven't seen in years, and bought rounds of drinks for complete strangers at some of my favorite hangouts. I've done everything I could to be noticed and remembered.

I've tried not to dwell on this meeting with the Russian killer, or on what I've paid him to do.

I've been keeping my eye on the local paper, television news stations and the internet, but there've been no reports on

Sara, or any other woman's unfortunate demise. Each night on my ride home I've been expecting to find police officers at my front door with an arrest warrant, but it never happened.

I sit across from Dmitri and nervously stare in his direction.

"Ah. Mr. Deputer." He raises his glass.

"Look, I'm in no mood for a toast. Is the job done?"

He doesn't say anything, but simply nods, reaches into his pocket and lays a photograph face down on the table. I reach out to grab it but he stops me.

"Are you sure you vant to look?"

"Yes and no." I can taste bile in my throat.

"This is not something ve can undo," he says while removing his hand from the photograph.

I glance nervously across the room, not sure I really want to flip the photograph over. I feel a sharp pain in my chest, as I slowly turn the picture over and stare at the gruesome mug shot of Sara with a large bullet hole in her forehead. Her eyes are wide open, staring back at me with a look of disbelief. Or accusation. I'm not sure which, but it's frightening.

I place both hands over my mouth as I feel moisture building in my eyes.

I whisper, "My God, what have I done?"

Dmitri's eyes shift from side to side and he whips the photograph off the table. His eyes are like laser beams as he stares at me. "This is vhat you vanted, no?"

Confused. So confused. All I can do is nod up and down and then slowly shake my head from side to side.

"I do vhat you ask."

I rub my eyes. "Is this real? How do I know this is real? How do I know that you really killed her? You could have just photoshopped a picture of her!"

I can't believe I'm having second thoughts. A part of me wishes this is all a scam and that Sara is still alive, but Dmitri sighs and says, "Look at *kartinki*, vhat you see? Vhat is missing?"

I force myself to stare at the photograph again, trying not to look into Sara's eyes. One of her earrings is missing, that's what he's talking about. It's one of the earrings I gave her on our fifth anniversary.

He sees the recognition in my eyes and says, "Ah, you see!" He slips his hand into his inside jacket pocket, then opens his fingers and shows me the missing earring sitting on his palm.

My heart sinks as the reality hits me. "Christ! You really did do it."

"You have money?"

I sit stunned, staring at him. "You're a cold bastard, aren't you?"

He smirks and asks again.

My mind is a million years away, remembering the day I asked Sara to marry me. It was the happiest day of my life.

"You have my money?" he asks again, stabbing me in the forehead with his right index finger to get my attention.

I nod, hand him the envelope under the table and watch it disappear.

He tosses back the dregs of his drink and then leans in close. He grabs my jacket lapel, pulls me towards him and I smell the whiskey on his hot breath.

His eyes are wild and sinister, and although his face sports a smile, it is the sneer of a cold-blooded son of a bitch.

His voice is a near whisper as he says, "If you tell anyone of this, I svear I vill kill you. Do you understand me? Your death vill not be quick like your pretty vife's, but it vill be slow and painful. Do you understand?"

I feel my lips move, but I can't get the words out.

"Do you fucking understand?" He is violently shaking me.

"Yes. Yes. Yes!" My head jerks up and down in a nod.

He taps my cheek. "Good little comrade."

He abruptly releases my jacket, and I collapse helplessly into the seat. Then he stands up and heads towards the exit. He opens the door and looks back at me, pointing two fingers towards his eyes, then points the same two fingers back at me before disappearing into the sunlight. The son of a bitch will be watching me.

My chin drops to my chest as I realize the magnitude of what I've done.

I try holding back the tears, but I can't.

What have I done? Dear God, what have I done?

I'm not supposed to feel this way. After all, she deserved what she got. Didn't she? *Didn't she?* As hard as I try, I can't hold back the tears and I begin sobbing. Behind all the burning jealousy and the anger, I'd forgotten how much I loved her and how wonderful my life had been with her in it. I was such an idiot for having cheated on her. She was the best thing that ever happened to me.

The bartender looks at me and points at the door.

I drop my head into my hands. "Sara my love. I'm so sorry. God forgive me. What the hell was I thinking? I love you. I've always loved you."

"Hey, buddy, get the hell out of here before I throw you out. All that blubbering is upsetting the clientele."

I want to punch the guy in the face, but what good will that do? It won't change what I've done. It won't bring my Sara back.

I wipe my eyes, stand up and stagger toward the front entrance hoping to make it outside before my legs give out and I puke all over the floor.

I stand outside the bar, thumping my forehead gently against the brick wall, repeating over and over again, "Oh my God. Oh my God. I don't think I can do this. I thought I could, but I don't think I can live with what I've done!"

I turn my back to the wall and slide down into a sitting position.

Tears run down my face; I slap the sides of my head with my fists. "What have I done? I'm so sorry baby. Shit, shit, shit. I'm so damn sorry!"

A young woman walking by stops and asks me if I'm okay.

I look up and for a moment I see Sara's face on this stranger. Is this how it's going to be for the rest of my life?

"No, I'm not okay. I've done something so awful I don't know if I can live with it."

"Whatever it is, I'm sure you'll find a way to be forgiven."

"I don't know about that. I just don't know."

"Sometimes all it takes is doing the right thing."

"The only right thing to do is to undo what I've done, but it's too late, there's no way to do that." My vocal cords feel like sandpaper.

I look up and she's gone. Disappeared into thin air.

I stand up, reach for my cell phone, and dial 911. I know it will not bring Sara back, but I realize it's the right thing to do, the only thing to do.

"Hello Police, I'd like to report a…"

Suddenly my body is jerked backwards and the cell phone is ripped out of my hand. I can't see my attacker, but someone's arm has me by the throat and drags me into the alley. I struggle but can't escape the firm grip as I'm thrown to the ground. My head strikes the pavement. Groggy and disoriented, my eyes come into focus and I recognize the face of Dmitri, standing over me.

He grabs me by the hair and says, "You stupid *durak*, I varned you."

In my peripheral vision I see something shiny, metallic, but I'm too weak and disoriented to stop what's about to happen. I feel the sharp, searing slash of the blade going across my neck and I instinctively grab my throat with both hands in a futile attempt to stop the bleeding.

I taste blood in my throat, and hear the gurgling sound as I attempt to swallow…

Dmitri stares down at me, snaps a photograph, dials my cell phone and holds it to his ear.

The last thing I hear before losing consciousness forever… is…

Remorse

"Hello Sara. Job is done."

No Return Address

Each year over a thousand mail carriers in the United States are attacked by dogs while delivering mail. It wouldn't be an overstatement to say that most mail carriers are leery about making deliveries to houses where dogs are running loose in the yard.

As mail carrier John Toro turns the corner onto Jefferson Avenue, he spots the rotund figure of Cecil Waters standing by his mailbox. People like Cecil Waters make the thought of confronting a dog in the yard almost desirable.

This is the third time this week that Toro has found Waters standing by his mailbox waiting to ambush him.

Toro stops his vehicle and stares in bemusement at the sad figure. Mr. Waters appears to be in his late fifties, with a receding hairline, a round protruding belly, and a pencil-thin mustache across his upper lip. His face has a pasty white complexion and he's wearing a blue bathrobe in need of a good washing.

He stumbles toward the vehicle, waving several envelopes in one hand while balancing a drink in the other.

Toro makes a quick attempt to defuse the tantrum he knows is coming his way.

"Well, good morning, Mr. Waters. It looks like it's going to be a Chamber of Commerce Day today."

"Don't 'good morning' me, Toro!" Waters replies. His hand shakes, spilling some of his drink down the front of his bathrobe.

Toro can see that even though it isn't quite 9:00 AM, Waters is already plastered.

"What the hell are you going to do about my mail?" the man demands, slapping the envelopes against the roof of the vehicle.

Toro pushes the truck door open, forcing Waters to step back.

"I know you're upset, Mr. Waters, but please allow me to get out of the vehicle, before you attack me with your accusations."

Waters gives him an angry look. "Attack you! Ha! That's rich. You'd have me arrested over something so trivial but won't do a damn thing about my mail!"

"Who said anything about having you arrested?" Toro replies, staring at the drink in Waters' hand. "I've already explained this to you, Mr. Waters. You and I both know there's nothing in the Postal Regulations that forbids people from sending mail without providing a return address. Whoever is sending you these letters is either playing a prank on you or paying you back for something you did to them. In either case it has nothing to do with me or the US Postal Service."

Waters steps back and stumbles off the curb, losing his balance.

Toro can see the rage in his eyes.

"Are you implying that some stranger is stuffing my mailbox with these foul letters and it's my fault?" Waters yells. "That's absolutely ridiculous!"

"Look. I have no idea why you're getting these letters," Toro says, handing Waters today's mail.

"I think you know something, but you're not telling me!"

"What are you talking about? That's crazy?" Toro shakes his head in frustration.

"It's harassment!" screams Waters. "I keep getting these nasty letters filled with obituary clippings of people I've never met! Why would someone do this to me? What have I done to deserve this?"

"You're asking the wrong person, Mr. Waters."

Waters releases a loud and foul-smelling belch.

Toro turns his head in disgust. "For Pete's sake, Mr. Waters, that is completely uncalled for. What makes you think that hitting the bottle at 9:00 in the morning is going to help you make sense of this situation?"

"I don't think how much I drink is any of your goddamn business!"

"Suit yourself, Mr. Waters." Toro turns toward his truck.

"Don't you walk away from me, young man! I demand an answer!"

Toro spins around to face Waters who jerks back and loses his balance again. Toro grabs his arm to keep him from falling on his rear.

"Look, *I* didn't send those letters! Do you understand? I don't know where you got this ridiculous idea in your head, but if you think it's me, go ahead and report me. I can prove my innocence."

Waters pulls his arm away, forcing Toro to release him.

"Now who's attacking who?" he says with a smug look on his face. "You're just paying me back because I reported you for not delivering my mail a couple of months ago."

Toro laughs. "I thought you'd be too embarrassed to ever bring that up again. After all, you're the one who went to the post office and asked us to put a hold on your mail. You told us you'd be out of town on vacation, but later had a change of plans. Sadly, you were too drunk to remember what you did and accused me of withholding your mail. You're the one who made a fool of yourself, not me. Why would I hold a grudge against you?"

An ugly smirk flashes across Waters' lips. "You might have fooled your employer, but you didn't fool me. I know you did it."

"I give up," Toro replies, flailing his arms in the air as if shooing away a fly.

"I'm going to report you to your superiors."

"Go ahead. If you believe these letters are some form of harassment on my part, then call the Postmaster General's office and report me. I have no idea what will happen, but that's not my problem, because I did not send the letters."

"Alright, if that's true, then I give you permission to stop delivering all letters to my house that don't have a return address."

"Okay, first you report me and accuse me of not delivering your mail, and now you have the audacity to ask me not to deliver your mail? What kind of drunken logic is that?"

"You can't speak to me that way. I pay your damn salary through my taxes. You damn well work for me!"

"Didn't you tell me you're a retired mail carrier?"

"Yes, yes," Waters replies, waving the mail in the air in dismissal.

"Then you know darn well that it's illegal for me to withhold mail. If I took it upon myself to withhold anyone's mail, that would be just as bad as stealing it."

A look of disgust crosses Waters face. "Who said anything about stealing mail? I said nothing about stealing."

Toro lowers his head in frustration. "It's a moot point, Mr. Waters. I won't withhold any of your mail. Why don't you just throw the letters out?"

"What do you mean?"

"Why do you bother opening them if they are so upsetting? You say you don't know these people—then just throw the letters away!"

"How the hell do I know there isn't something important in there? If I don't see the damn things, I won't have to worry about it! You know the old saying: Out of sight, out of mind!"

"I told you, I can't —"

Waters rolls his eyes, so Toro stops in mid-sentence and turns toward his truck.

"Who the hell is doing this to me?" Waters shouts, oblivious to the fact that Toro is leaving.

"No idea. Not my problem! End of conversation. Enjoy the rest of your day, sir!"

As the mail truck pulls away, Waters screams after it, "And it wasn't my idea to retire! The bastards forced me to!"

Waters watches Toro's vehicle come to a screeching halt at the stop sign at the end of the street, then turn left onto Fountain Lawn Road and disappear into thin air.

Waters squints and whispers, "I must be seeing things." He raises his glass to his mouth, in one quick motion dumps the last few drops of bourbon down his throat and tosses the remaining ice cubes across his dry, weed-infested lawn.

He sifts through the newly delivered mail as he stumbles towards his house.

"That SOB handed me three new letters, all without return addresses. You're a damn liar, Toro." He slams the front door behind him.

He snatches the letter opener off the desk in the foyer, slits open the envelopes, and stares at the latest collection of clippings.

Mrs. Ronda Pine, 31, of Town Midland, FL.

Mr. Joseph Bender, 52, of Delton City, MA.

Mr. Samuel Burton, 47, of Winston Creek, CA.

His shaky hands add the latest round of obituary clippings to the ones already laid out on the dining room table. He runs his hands over his balding forehead and stares at each name.

"Who the hell are you people?" he says, grabbing his left arm to still the sharp pain shooting through it.

He has no idea why anyone would do this to him. After all those years of delivering mail, the town and area names where the deceased lived are familiar to him, but the faces and names mean nothing.

The familiar sharp jab in his lower back reminds him that it's time for another round of pain meds. In the kitchen he pours himself another drink to wash down the pills. He walks back into the dining room, sits in a chair and waits for the pain to subside.

He rubs his eyes and stares at the obituary clippings, the faces of complete strangers staring back at him. His eyelids grow heavy as he takes another sip of bourbon.

The dream is back.

It's a cold November morning, and he hears the sound of that large, black and white nasty mutt barking as it attacks his pants cuff. He turns to kick the mutt, loses his balance, and falls over little Johnny Blum's tricycle. Excruciating pain shoots up his rear end.

In the strange way of dreams, it's weeks later, and he's been forced into early retirement because the pain of his broken pelvis hasn't gone away even after extensive therapy. He's at the part where he is opening the garden gate, a knife in his hand to slit that mutt's throat, when the dream is interrupted..."

Waters lifts his head, wipes his eyes, and sees Randy Cooms, his neighbor from across the street, tapping on the front window.

"Mr. Waters, are you okay?" Waters shakes his head to regain his composure, lifts his sore body from the chair, and drags himself over to the front door, pulling it open with a creak.

Cooms stares at him with a look of concern. "Mr. Waters, are you alright? I rang the door bell several times, but you didn't answer, so I peeked in the window. It almost looked like you were trying to stab at something in the air. Is everything okay?"

"I'm fine, Officer Cooms. I just took my meds and must have dozed off."

"Can I come in for a moment?"

Waters grunts and grudgingly opens the door wider.

"That must have been some dream you were having."

"I don't remember any of my dreams," replies Waters in a dismissive tone. "Can I fix you a drink?"

Cooms lets out a sigh. "Ah, it's 10:00 in the morning! Bit too early for me. Besides, I'm on duty in an hour."

Waters takes his drink and carefully sits back down in his chair. "So, what can I do for you, Cooms?"

Cooms holds up a handwritten note. "I believe you left this note on my door?"

It takes a moment before Waters remembers placing a note on Cooms door the night before.

"Yes, of course I did."

"It sounded pretty urgent, so I thought I'd drop by before I leave for the Station. So, what can I do for you?"

"I'm being harassed!"

"Harassed? Harassed by whom?"

"No idea."

An irritated smile crosses Cooms face, as if to say, *Seriously?*

"Harassed in what way, Mr. Waters?"

Waters points at the clipping on the table. "Dead people keep showing up in my mailbox."

The look on Cooms' face turns serious. "Is this some kind of joke? How much have you been drinking this morning, Mr. Waters?"

"This has nothing to do with me drinking. Why are people always telling me what I can or can't do with my own damn time?"

"I don't care what you do in your own home, but you're not making any sense."

Waters points at the photos again. "What part of 'dead people keep showing up in my mailbox' don't you understand?"

Cooms looks at his watch. "I don't have time for this, Mr. Waters, so please tell me what's going on?"

"For the last week, I've been receiving anonymous letters with obituary clippings inside and I have no idea why. My lying-ass mail carrier insists he has nothing to do with this, but I don't think he's being truthful, because the envelopes have no return address on them."

"Return address? What are you talking about? What does that have to do with anything?"

"That's what I want you to find out!"

"Do you have reason to believe that the postal carrier has something against you?"

"No."

Cooms stares down at the clippings. "None of these people are familiar to you?"

"Nope!" replies Waters, letting out a belch.

"Have you received any threatening phone calls, emails or letters?"

Waters points at the clippings. "These aren't threatening enough?"

Cooms scratches his head. "These are certainly odd, but the clippings alone don't qualify as harassment. This could be someone playing a practical joke. Do you know anyone who'd have a reason to do that?"

Waters shakes his head, then walks out of the room. He gets a fresh glass of whiskey, comes back into the living room, and belches again. He can see by the scowl on Cooms face that he doesn't approve of his drinking habit.

Waters points his glass at Cooms. "You have no right to judge me. You have no idea the damn pain I'm in and what I've been through these last few years."

"You're a grown man, Mr. Waters, you can do whatever you want, but if you're asking my advice, I suggest you get yourself a part time job, a hobby or something. I saw my old man go through this same thing after he retired. I know the signs. If you don't do something about this, I assure you that your life will end poorly."

Waters smiles and says, "Thanks for the sermon, Cooms, but I don't need your advice. And more importantly, what does that have to do with my immediate problem?"

Cooms shakes his head and laughs. "What problem? Just throw the photos away and contact me if you receive a real threat. Until then take care of yourself."

Waters ignores the last comment. "What I hear you saying is that there's nothing you can do about this. Some sick bastard is sending me clippings of dead people and there's nothing you can do to stop it."

"It's a sad joke, but it's not illegal. Therefore, there is nothing I can do about it."

Waters places his glass down, clutches his own arm and wiggles his fingers. There is a scowl on his face.

"So, this is the kind of shitty service I receive from government agencies… I pay your damn salary through my taxes. What kind of sh—."

"Mr. Waters? Are you okay?"

Waters closes his eyes and grabs hold of the table. A look of pain comes over his face.

"I'm fine. I sometimes get a shooting pain down my arm and numbness in my fingers. It's probably just a side effect of all the medication I'm taking."

"You don't look good, Mr. Waters. I think you need to see a doctor and get that checked out as soon as possible. It looks like you might be working toward a stroke. You need help."

Waters picks up his drink and takes a big gulp. "What the hell do you know? You're not a doctor—you're a police officer, and a lousy one too! Get out of my damn house!"

"That's not fair, Mr. Waters. I'm only trying to help you."

"Get the hell out!" Waters spins away from Cooms, loses his balance and drops to the floor. His arm is throbbing and the pain has moved into his chest. The last thing he hears before losing consciousness is Officer Cooms telling him he's calling 911.

* * *

Waters wakes up in a dark room, lit only by a single longneck lamp. The type of lamp that you see used in interrogation rooms in old movies. The air smells foul, like the stench of burnt palmetto palms in a Florida brush fire. He notices that his arms and legs are free, but when he tries to move them they won't budge.

Panic shoots through him. "Hello!" he screams. "I'm awake! Where am I? I can't move my damn arms or legs. Is anybody here? Can anyone help me?"

He hears someone cough and the sound of footsteps coming toward him. Out of the darkness, a man appears wearing medical scrubs, but his unkempt red beard and New York Yankees baseball cap and the lit cigarette hanging from his lips seem out of place for a medical doctor in a hospital room.

"Hello, Mr. Waters. How are you feeling? Are you in pain?"

"No, but I can't move my legs or arms. I'm paralyzed. Who are you? Where the hell am I?"

The man looks at Waters, blows smoke in the air, and then smiles. "Don't worry, Mr. Waters, we'll take care of that soon enough!"

"Take care of what?"

"The pain."

Waters is furious. "I demand to know who you are and where I am. Tell me or I'll have to speak to your superior."

The man grins and scratches his bearded chin. "Oooh!" he says. "Guess I better tell you. I wouldn't want to get into trouble."

"Are you mocking me?"

"Of course not, Mr. Waters, that would be mean, wouldn't it? Well, if you must know, you're at Purgatory General and my name is Dr. Howl, but my friends call me Red."

"Purgatory General? There's no such place! You're making this up. I demand the truth. Where am I?"

Dr. Howl sighs. "You have no idea how many times I've heard that."

"Heard what?"

"That Purgatory General doesn't exist."

Waters is confused. "You're lying, Doctor. I demand to speak to your supervisor!"

"Relax, Mr. Waters. Would you mind if I take your temperature?"

"Do I have a freakin' choice?" Waters watches the doctor's hand come down toward his face.

Pain sears across his forehead, and he screams. Dr. Howl laughs and removes his hand.

"Jesus! Your hand feels like a red-hot cattle prod!" Waters says.

Dr. Howl grins and replies in a mocking tone, "So sorry, Mr. Waters. I've been told that I run a little hot; guess that's why they call me Red! Get it?"

"Well, Red, keep your damn hands off me," Waters replies, feeling panicked. "How did I get here?"

"Gabriel and Michael brought you."

"Gabriel? Michael? Who the hell are they?"

"I'm Gabriel," says a voice, then a figure steps out of the darkness into the light.

"And I'm Michael." Another figure comes into the light.

Waters recognizes the faces. "Cooms? Toro? Is this some kind of joke?"

"This is no joke, Mr. Waters." Gabriel's tone is serious.

"God, Cooms, I'm so glad you're here. I need help."

"Well, isn't that precious!" says Dr. Howl, then he bursts into an eerie high-pitched laugh.

Waters looks a Gabriel. "Officer Cooms," he pleads, frightened, "you need to arrest this man. He's done something to me... I can't move my arms or legs. I think he's crazy and I'm not even sure he's a real doctor."

"Calm down, Mr. Waters," Gabriel replies, "he's not about to hurt you—"

Dr. Howl bends over and says in Waters' ear, "Well, not yet anyway."

Waters screams in horror. "Please get me out of here, Officer Cooms! He just threatened to hurt me. You heard him!"

"I'm afraid it's not that simple, Cecil. Only you have the power to set yourself free."

"What the heck are you talking about, Cooms? I can't move! How am I supposed to set myself free?"

Michael leans forward over Waters and lays his hands on his shoulders. "You must repent in order to be set free!"

"Repent for what? I've done nothing wrong, Toro. Get your hands off me."

Gabriel gives him a look that says, 'You and I know better than that.' "You must repent for all the things you've done wrong in your life. For all the times you've harmed others."

"Harmed others? What the hell are you talking about, Cooms? I've been a model citizen. This is ridicul—"

"Really?" pipes in Michael. "And what about all those times you've stolen money from birthday and anniversary cards while you were delivering the mail?"

"That accusation was never proven, Toro. Who the hell asked for your opinion?"

"What about the girls in Seattle and Los Angeles you raped when you were on a drug-induced bender in your twenties?"

"Complete lies. It was my word against theirs. I was never charged with a crime."

Gabriel shakes his head and says, "What about the young boy you took advantage of, when you were babysitting your friend's children?"

"How dare you accuse me of something so disgusting! I did no such thing! I will have them take away your damn badge for that accusation, Officer Cooms!"

Michael stands over Waters. "Perhaps you've forgotten the fact that you allowed your mother to die by withholding her medications? Was she too much of a burden for you to handle, Mr. Waters?"

Waters feels like his eyes are about to pop out of his head.

"You son of a bitch! I knew all along you sent those clippings, Toro! You bastard, I didn't do any of the things you guys are accusing me of doing! You're both liars and poor excuses for human beings!"

Dr. Howl laughs. "Human beings? Good one, Mr. Waters."

Waters doesn't hear him. "I will never confess to the things you claim I've done. Never! I'll have your damn heads. You hear me! Your careers!"

"I believe the gentleman protests too much," laughs Dr. Howl.

Gabriel and Michael huddle together in the corner, until Dr. Howl interrupts them.

"Why do you guys bother? Seriously, people like Waters here have selective amnesia. You've seen it a million times. Why would you expect them to repent? They've enjoyed committing every one of your so-called sins and they obviously show no signs of regret!"

Gabriel decides to give Waters one last opportunity. "Everyone deserves a second chance, Mr. Waters. Everyone deserves to be forgiven."

Dr. Howl laughs out loud. "Even me, Gabriel?"

Gabriel glances at the Doctor and grins. "Well, maybe not everyone!"

Gabriel waits for Waters to respond, but the man turns away and ignores him.

Dr. Howl walks behind Michael and Gabriel and pats both of them on the back. "Okay, fellows, I think you got your answer. You guys gave it your best shot. Now pardon my language, dear brothers, but why don't you both fly the hell out of here? You can't win them all."

Gabriel and Michael raise their hands towards Waters in a benediction. "God bless you, Cecil Waters. Remember that nothing was unforgiveable, except the fact that you refuse to acknowledge the wrongs you have done and to ask for forgiveness."

Suddenly, a large hole appears in the ceiling, and a brilliant light shines down upon them. A light so bright that Waters is forced to close his eyes.

The sound of a loud booming voice engulfs the room. "Mr. Waters has made his choice. Come home, my Sons."

The ominous tone of those words forces Waters' eyes open, and he stares in disbelief as Cooms and Toro sprout wings and disappear into the light.

Dr. Howl smiles, looks over a Waters and flicks his head. "Pretty dramatic stuff, eh?"

Waters stares back at the Doctor, stunned. "How in the hell did they do that?"

"You thought that was cool? You ain't seen nothing yet!"

Dr. Howl points at Waters, crooks his finger, motioning for him to come closer, and for the first time Waters notices the long black pointed fingernails on the doctor's hands and the wild evil glow in his eyes.

Dr. Howl lets out a wicked laugh. "Come, my child. Adolf, Mao, Pol Pot, and Uncle Joe await you."

A feeling of sheer terror fills Waters. "I'm not your damn chi—"

The last thing Dr. Howl sees of him is two blood-covered arms shooting up through the mattress and pulling him down into a burning pit of fire.

Left alone in silence, Dr. Howl grins, takes one last puff on his cigarette and whispers, "Even after all these years, the feeling of victory never gets old."

Hell to Pay

It begins as just another workday. I arrive at my desk at 4:15 in the morning, drop my briefcase on the floor and head for the coffeemaker. I have always loved this quiet time of the morning before the rest of the staff arrives and the hustle and bustle of a major newspaper kicks into action.

My name is Jason Garrett and I'm one of several reporters who cover the crime beat for the *News-Tribune*. I have a couple of potential stories in the works, nothing I can sink my teeth into just yet. I'm waiting for a source to verify some of my information.

Coffee in hand, I weave around the maze of cubicles and arrive back at my desk and immediately notice the manila envelope sitting there. I'm a bit surprised that I didn't spot it before because my name is neatly handwritten on its face.

MR. JASON GARRETT

SENIOR CRIME REPORTER - NEWS-TRIBUNE

The postmark is dated February 14th, three days ago. I carefully slit open the envelope using the fancy letter opener my mother gave me when I began my career at the *News-Tribune* twelve years ago. I remember the pride on her face as she watched me unwrap it and place it on my new desk. As a single mom, she had worked extremely hard to finance my educational needs, which had culminated in a journalism degree and a great job. For that, I will be forever grateful to a wonderful, loving mother and to all the great teachers along the way.

Inside the envelope I find a ten-page letter from someone named Mildred Cruickshank. I have no idea who Ms. or Mrs. Cruickshank is, but apparently, she knows me from my writing. The letter begins innocently enough, but quickly weaves a fascinating story about loneliness, hate, revenge, and murder.

Dear Mr. Garrett,

Although we've never formally met, I'm a huge fan of your investigative reporting and I feel that I can trust you to tell my story with truth and compassion.

My name is Mildred Cruickshank and I'm a former resident of the Royal Arms Apartment on the south side of town.

Hmmm – the Royal Arms Apartment rings a bell, I think. Wait! Isn't that the building that burned down several days ago? Former resident, indeed.

I worked as an investment advisor at Donnelly Investments for 30 years until my forced retirement two years ago. I was very good at my job and over the years made millions of dollars for many of my clients, but like others in my profession, I didn't see the downturn in the economy coming and ended up with huge losses to my clients' portfolios. The company was very nice about offering me a retirement package and told all my clients that I was moving on to bigger and better things, but it was a lie. I was actually given an ultimatum to leave quietly or face a humiliating termination.

Sadly, there are no secrets in the investment business. Everyone knew the truth about my retirement, making it impossible for me to find someone willing to hire me under those circumstances.

It was a very humbling experience to go from being on top of the world making a six-figure salary and living in a downtown penthouse to working as a lowly credit counselor for a not-for-profit firm and living in a low-income apartment like the Royal Arms. What most people don't know is that the market crash also affected my personal investments. To put it kindly, I came out of the crash dead broke. The settlement offer from Donnelly's, although generous, didn't last very long and it was pretty much exhausted when my foolish pride kept me from moving out of the penthouse even though I knew I could no longer afford to live there.

As if that weren't enough, my husband Rex left me for another sugar baby. I had always suspected that Rex had married me for my money, but it was still a shock when he proved my suspicions correct. Rex was and is a very handsome man twelve years my junior who wooed me on one of my rare Bahamas vacations. I should have known the marriage wouldn't last, but the guy was such a hunk, and the sex was fantastic.

"Geez, lady, I was feeling sorry for you until you knowingly married this loser," I say out loud.

Rex was a good guy but couldn't hold a job if his life depended on it. I was too busy with my successful career to care about Rex's lack of employment, and I sure didn't need his income to keep me happy. Rex used me as his sugar baby, and he was my sex toy. That was the true nature of the relationship, and I should have known that he wouldn't stick around once the money was gone. The last I heard, he was bunking with a 55-year-old department store heiress in Malibu.

I just celebrated my 60th birthday last week (Rex is 47), so I'd like to believe that I lost him to a younger woman and that money had nothing to do with it.

A younger woman with a shitload of money, I think as a smile crosses my face. I guess ole Rex isn't as dumb as I thought.

The sound of chatter slowly fills the room as some of my co-workers start drifting in to work.

Faced with the prospect of downsizing everything in my life, I decided to move back to the comfort of my old neighborhood and into the Royal Arms, which when it was new was considered upscale living.

The years have not been kind to the old girl, and the Arms is now a low-income, rent-controlled apartment owned by someone who can best be described as a slumlord. The four-story building still has all the charming characteristics it had in its heyday, but now everything is dirty, run down and in desperate need of repairs.

The once beautiful globe lights in the lobby are filthy, some are broken, and every other one doesn't light up. The wood inlay that decorates the elevator is carved with graffiti and the walls are plastered with the frustrations of illiterate poets and want-to-be artists. Even the gold-colored ornate mailboxes are held shut with large padlocks.

The wallpaper in the hallways is stained and peeling in many places, the floors are dirty, and the carpets should have been replaced a decade ago.

As I read this, I can't help but think that perhaps the fire is the best thing that could have happened to this dump. I'm always amazed that there are so many people in this affluent city still living in such unsanitary conditions.

It wasn't easy for someone of my once high stature to stoop to this level, but what choice did I have? I was flat broke and working a job that barely covered my food and rent for the month.

Fortunately, the apartments are spacious, enough to fit all my beautiful furniture (something I refused to give up in downsizing) and make for a cozy oasis in a desert of dust.

The Royal Arms is a four-story building comprised of four apartments on each floor. I'm on the fourth floor in unit 4D and I'm considered the new kid on the block. The other units are occupied by what I would call 'lifers', people who move in and stay their whole lives. Mrs. Halper in 1D is a housewife whose husband was in the dry-cleaning business but died years ago. Mr. Solomon in 2D is a retired doorman who rarely leaves his apartment.

I have the misfortune of living across from apartment 3D, which is occupied by Sandra Nuesense and her 16-year-old terrors, Randy and Teddy. She's an unemployed drunk who survives on her welfare checks and her boys can only be described as juvenile delinquents.

Randy is the quiet one, but if you look deeply into his eyes, you can see the hatred and frustration of an undisciplined youth. Teddy, his bipolar twin, is completely unpredictable and just plain scary.

I made my acquaintance with the brothers on my third day in the building while riding the elevator up to my floor. The one boy, whom I would come to know as Randy, was staring at the centerfold of a Playboy *magazine while his brother Teddy carved foul language on the elevator wall. I knew that I should keep my mouth shut, but that is just not who I am, so I told him to please stop damaging the walls.*

Randy lowered his magazine, looked at me as if I were crazy and said, "Who the fu_ _ are you?" (I refuse to stoop to their level, so I will censor their disgusting language. I'm sure you'll be able to fill in the blanks.)

Teddy turned, took the sharp object he was using to carve the graffiti, pointed it at my face and said, "Mind your fu_ _ _ _ g business, grandma, or next time I'll shove this up your ass."

I was shocked as they both laughed and did what athletes would call a 'high five'. The flicker of hatred that crossed Teddy's eyes was so intense that it frightened me because I knew that he meant every word.

I remember running from the elevator and trying to unlock my apartment door, but my hands were shaking so badly that I couldn't get the key to work. The twins walked by and one of them patted me on the behind and asked if I needed help, then I heard them laugh as I rushed into my apartment. I sat on my sofa, shaken, as my cat Mr. Tinkles jumped on my lap to comfort me.

As you might imagine, this was only the first of many unpleasant encounters I had with the Nuesense twins.

A week later I discovered Mrs. Halper sitting in the hallway outside her apartment crying. When I asked her what was wrong, she said the twins had accosted her in the elevator and taken her grocery money for the week. I felt so bad for her that I gave her forty dollars (money I couldn't afford to give away) so she could buy food.

I was so upset that I pounded on the Nuesenses' door until an ill-looking, foul-smelling woman answered. I assumed it was Mrs. Nuesense and I gave her a piece of my mind. She leaned against the door frame and listened to me telling her how disrespectful her sons had been towards me and other tenants in the building and what they had done to Mrs. Halper. I assured her that if this continued, I would involve the police.

She laughed and said, "Go ahead. You think I give a shit? In fact, you'd be doing me a big favor, so go ahead call the cops. I ain't got no control over them boys. Get the cops involved, but don't expect me to tattle on my boys. I gotta live with 'em and I ain't stirring up trouble for myself. Do you hear me?"

"How can you live like this?" I asked.

"Like what?" she replied.

"In fear of your own kids," I said. "If you know they're doing wrong, then you need to speak up."

"Listen, lady, speaking up could get me killed, and that ain't about to happen. I suggest you keep your trap shut if you know what's good for you," she said as she slammed the door in my face.

Oh my God, I think, now there's a real treasure. I peek at the clock and notice it's almost five in the morning. The noise level in the room has picked up considerably, but I ignore it in order to finish reading the letter before my six o'clock staff meeting. The more I read, the more I see the makings of a great article for the evening edition.

I was so frustrated and upset, but neither Mrs. Halper nor the Nuesense woman was willing to speak to the police, so I decided to let it go.

Everything was fine over the next few days. I didn't see or hear a peep from the Nuesense twins. Then one morning, I was taking the garbage to the disposal chute, and they appeared out of nowhere and blocked the hallway in both directions.

Randy was wearing a cut-off t-shirt and dirty jeans. He had a new tattoo on his left arm which read 'Motherf_ _ _ _ _' and he waved his finger at me saying, "Momma says you're going to call the cops on us. Is that true?"

"Why would she say something like that?" I replied, playing dumb.

"She told us we better cool it if we didn't want trouble from the neighbors," added Teddy, "but she wouldn't tell us which neighbor until I held her hand over the gas burner until she squealed."

Randy giggled and moved closer.

"Why would you do that to your own mother? What kind of animal are you? She carried you around for nine months and this is how you treat her?"

"Is there anything worse than a self-righteous bitch?" Teddy said to Randy.

Teddy snorted and moved closer. I was seconds from screaming when I heard a voice say, "Is there a problem here?"

We all turned and saw Mr. Gonzolo, the superintendent, standing in the hallway carrying a large wrench.

"I came up to fix Mr. Solomon's clogged drain and I see this," he said, pointing at us with the wrench. "Now I ask you again, is there a problem here?"

Randy and Teddy turned away and headed towards their apartment, but not before whispering, "You're one lucky bitch. This ain't over, lady."

I thanked Mr. Gonzolo and told him what had happened. He was very sympathetic and told me to stay away from those boys, because they were nothing but trouble. I asked why he hadn't called the police on the boys, and he told me he had, several times, but they were underage, and all the cops did was talk to them. It was very frustrating because he was sure they had committed vandalism in the building, but everyone was so frightened of them that no one would testify against them. Everyone was afraid they'd be let out again with just a warning and then there would be hell to pay.

I'm frustrated just reading the letter; I can only imagine what it was like for the people in that building. It's a bit disturbing, but in my profession, I see it often: people who are too afraid to step forward and help take some of these deviants off the street. It only seems to happen after the problem has escalated to the point where somebody gets hurt before people will do something about it.

The following week I had an appointment with my specialist. The cancer in my lungs had returned and she wanted to prepare me for another round of chemo. Forty years of smoking, poor nutrition and a stressful career had taken its toll on my health and the prognosis for recovery was not particularly good. I felt frightened, upset and alone as I exited the elevator and noticed my apartment door was half open. I know I should have called the police immediately, but I was concerned about Mr. Tinkles, so I entered cautiously. The place was a mess, my furniture was knocked over, there was hateful graffiti painted on the walls and my sofa cushions had been slashed. I ran to the cupboard where I had my spending money stashed in a metal container, but it was empty. I began crying and calling Mr. Tinkles' name, but there was no response. Down the hallway I noticed the blood and I knew that what I'd find in the bedroom was going to break my heart. There I found Mr. Tinkles dead on the bed. I screamed and cried so loud that Mr. Gonzolo heard me on the first floor and called 911.

I put the letter down and wipe the moisture from my eyes. I don't even know the woman, but at this moment I'm filled with sadness. I compose myself and continue reading.

The week after the terrible incident is a complete blur. I remember speaking to the police, I recall accusing the boys of committing the crime and I know that the boys were taken in for questioning, but most of all I remember the pain and anger I felt when I had my sweet baby Mr. Tinkles cremated.

As I held his urn against my chest, I felt the sadness of knowing I would never see him again, but a small part of me was relieved that I wouldn't have to abandon him to strangers when my illness took its final course. It would have been difficult to give him up and even more difficult to find someone who would have loved him as much as I did.

The boys were never charged. No witnesses came forward and no evidence was found in the apartment linking them to the crime. Their mother swore that they never left her apartment all day that day, so they were released with a strong warning that the police had them on their radar.

I thought about moving, but where could this sick, old, broken woman go? I had no choice but to move on with my life, what little life remained. The insurance company replaced my furniture and the stolen money, but no one could repair my anger and my broken heart.

What I'm about to tell you will probably change your opinion of me for the worst, but I harbor no hard feelings and have no remorse for my actions.

I have always hated guns, but after the ordeal, I purchased a gun and paid for lessons on how to use it properly.

"Oh, boy, I'm not sure I like where this is headed," I mutter to myself.

I've never been a violent woman, but the circumstances in my life and my poor health made me realize that I could not die without the justice I felt I deserved. I'm not a deeply religious woman, but I hope that my God is truly a forgiving one.

The twins laid low for a while, but as time went on and people went back to their everyday lives, the terrible twins went back to doing what they do best. I began to hear stories about apartment break-ins and neighbors being accosted in the halls and the elevator.

My health had deteriorated in the past few months, and I knew that I would have to do what needed to be done sooner rather than later. The boys and I had done a good job of avoiding each other, but today we found each other riding the same elevator. They smiled at me and asked how my cat was doing. The smiles disappeared from their faces when I stuck the gun against Teddy's forehead and told him to let me know when he sees him.

Randy said, "You're making a big mistake, lady."

"Not as big as the one you made, son," I said, smiling. "Now walk out of this elevator and into my apartment. If you or your brother make a sound, I will shoot you dead right where you stand."

"You do that and you'll spend the rest of your fu_ _ _ _ g life in prison," said Teddy defiantly.

"I'm dying anyway, Teddy. Do you think I give a shit about going to prison?" (Sorry about the language, Mr. Garrett)

I know that it shouldn't, but reading her apology brings a smile to my face.

For the first time, the boys knew I was serious and began to show signs of fear on their faces. Their cocky attitude became subdued as they entered the apartment and began to ask what I was going to do to them.

"I'm going to tie you to those chairs," I said, "Randy, I want you to take that duct tape and tape your brother's ankles, wrists, legs, and waist to the chair. I just need to talk to you, and I want to make sure you don't leave before I say what needs to be said." I hated lying to them, but the truth would not garner their cooperation.

They looked at me with suspicion but did what they were told. What choice did they have? Die now or listen to this crazy old lady and maybe figure out a way to escape. If only they knew that there was no escape.

After restraining his brother, I had Randy tape his ankles and legs to the chair, and I taped his waist and wrists.

"Say what you have to say and then let us the f_ _k out of here," said Teddy.

"First, I would like you to apologize for killing Mr. Tinkles and destroying my apartment."

Teddy spit at me and replied, "F_ _k you! We ain't apologizing for something we didn't do."

"Such a foul mouth," I said as I covered it with a strip of duct tape. "What about you, Randy?"

"If you hurt my f_ _k_ _' brother, I'll kill you."

"Randy, Randy, Randy," I said as I taped his mouth and patted the side of his face. "No one will miss you or your crazy brother after you're gone."

They looked at each other and their eyes filled with fear. They began to cry and moan, rocking their chairs back and forth until both chairs fell over.

This is where I say goodbye, Mr. Garrett. In order to get this letter to you, I will have to tell you what I'm about to do and then drop this letter in the mailbox before I do it.

I will complete this letter, seal it, stamp it and drop it in the mailbox across the street. Before I mail it, I will close all the windows and turn on all of the gas burners on the stove and when I return to the building, I will pull the fire alarm and give all my neighbors enough time to leave the building before I re-enter my apartment and strike up my lighter.

A lifelong smoker perishing at the hands of her own cigarette lighter. Poetic justice, don't you agree?

I wish you a long and happy life, Mr. Garrett. Be kind to this tired old woman when you tell my story.

Best Regards,

Mildred Cruickshank

I place the letter down on my desk as the title of the article I'm about to write pops into my head. *HELL TO PAY – The Mildred Cruickshank Story.*

I hear my editor yelling at me from across the room. I'm late for the morning meeting.

I respond by saying, "Hey, boss, have I got a story for you."

Elevated Madness

*This story was included in the Writers @ Work – Collection
(Florida Writers Association), 2019*

The elevator stops and opens on the main lobby floor. A short, stubby young man with headphone wires coming out of both ears steps inside. He selects the twentieth floor, and melts into the back corner of the elevator.

I hear loud rock music escaping from his ear buds as the door squeaks and grinds shut.

Most days, he turns towards me and makes eye contact just long enough to acknowledge my presence, then returns to his music. Today, he surprises me by yanking off his ear buds, pointing his finger and saying, "Hey man. I know you!"

"That's not surprising," I reply with a smile on my face, "we see each other almost every day in this elevator."

"No, man. That's not what I mean. Aren't you the writer dude, the one who has his photograph posted on the bulletin board in my break room?"

"Ah yes. You're probably right. I have one posted in the break rooms on almost every floor."

He extends his hand toward me; I accept it and give him a solid shake.

"This is freaking awesome, man."

"Thanks," I reply, not knowing how to respond to his enthusiastic outburst. "My name is John Malpaso, but you know that already. What's yours?"

"Ringo," he says. "So John, what kind of stuff do you write?"

"Mostly short stories," I reply.

"Do you sell a lot of books?"

I grimace. "To tell you the truth, Ringo, I'd be lying if I said I did."

"Really?" There is a perplexed look on his face. "Aren't you any good?"

Wow, this guy's got a lot of nerve. "I'm an independent author who works a full-time job, so it's a struggle to get noticed."

He nods, but doesn't appear interested in my answer, because out of the blue he asks, "Have you ever met Stephen King?"

What the heck? How did we get from questioning my ability as a writer to meeting Stephen King?

"No, I've never met him."

I notice the look of disappointment, so I turn the conversation back to him. "What kind of books do you enjoy reading?"

"Me?" he answers, as if surprised by the question. "I'm not really into books."

"Really? No books at all?" I reply, dumbfounded by his answer.

"Nope. I don't enjoy reading."

"Wow!" I scratch my head. "So, you don't like reading, but you're a Stephen King fan. Okay! How does that work?"

"Duh! I've watched every one of his movies… scary stuff."

"Ah, his movies," I'm unable to keep my eyes from rolling up into my forehead.

I notice we just passed the fifteenth floor and can't help thinking that the twentieth floor can't get here fast enough. Seconds later the bell dings, indicating we've arrived.

Ringo gives me a thumbs up, pops the plugs back into his ears and steps out of the elevator. I smile and shake my head in amazement as the door begins to close. Suddenly, Ringo reaches back, grabs the door, and keeps it from closing.

"Forget something?" I ask.

He removes one ear bud and asks, "Are you by any chance working on a new book?"

Seriously! The nerve of this guy! "What difference does it make if I am or I'm not? You don't like books, so what would be the point of answering your silly question?"

The look can't hide his disappointment in my response.

"Sorry, John, I didn't mean to bother you with my 'silly question'," he says in a sarcastic tone of voice. Then he releases the door.

"Damn." I whisper. *I must have sounded like a total asshole. I run into this guy on a daily basis, and I don't want there to be any weirdness between us.*

I reach out, stop the elevator door just before it closes and step out into the hallway. Ringo is already halfway down the hall. I walk quickly, catch up to him and tap him on the shoulder.

He spins around and pulls out his ear buds. "What do you want?"

"I want to apologize. What I said was out of line. I need to be a little more understanding if I want to make my living as a writer. I can't take everything so personally."

I extend my hand in a gesture of friendship and wait for him to accept it.

He reaches out to shake it, then pulls his hand back and says, "Let me give you some advice. If you want to be a real writer, you might want to think about taking some sensitivity training classes and learn some humility."

This guy is freaking unbelievable! I think. *If I were a comic book character, there would be fire shooting out both ears right about now.* "Sure I'll take sensitivity classes, if you learn to read... you illiterate a-hole!"

I turn and walk away.

He shouts down the hallway, "Don't put words in my mouth! I never said I was illiterate, I just don't like reading!"

I stop and spin around to face him in the distance. "Normally, I'd say that whether or not you choose to read is your prerogative, but under the circumstances, don't you think it even a little bit strange that you started this conversation and you don't even read? What kind of psycho does that?"

"Psycho? Dude, if you must know, the only reason I brought up the subject is because my older brother Dan is the president of ABC Publishing up in New York City."

"Well whoop-dee-doo! Big freaking deal. What's that to me?"

"Wow. Here I was thinking that maybe I could hook you guys up, but you blew it *Mister* Malpaso. Have a nice day and good luck selling your crappy books!"

"Crappy books?" I reply, as his words suddenly sink in.

He smiles, plugs back in and walks off.

I slap the palm of my hand against my forehead. *Me and my damn temper. Why do I keep doing this to myself?*

Dejected, I walk back to the elevator and tap the "Up" button. The door opens and I toss my briefcase into the empty elevator in frustration, then shuffle in after it, tap the button to my floor and slump against the wall as the elevator goes up.

I step out on the 22nd floor and walk towards Suite 2210.

My assistant Marlie looks up as I enter the office.

"Good morning, Doctor. Your first appointment is in fifteen minutes, and the patient is already here. Is there anything I can get you?"

"Let me grab some coffee and a Tylenol. I'll buzz you when I'm ready."

"Sure, Doctor Malpaso. By the way, Dr. Windsor called to remind you about your keynote speech for next week's Anger Management Conference. He sounded worried that you might not be ready?"

I smile. "Not a problem, Marlie." Then I turn away and whisper under my breath, "But after what just happened, I'm thinking of changing the title to – *Physician Heal Thyself!*"

The Butcher

Henry hates when she watches the evening news. He says nothing good can come from watching sensationalized stories about murder, assault, robbery, traffic accidents and death. The world is filled with evil people, and he doesn't want that evil to enter the safety of his home.

Andrea knows Henry's heart is in the right place, but as a stay-at-home wife whose responsibilities involve cleaning house, cooking and dog-sitting Rottweilers, her life without the evening news felt boring and isolated. It was understood that once they got married, she would be expected to stay home and take care of the house while Henry worked and supported the family. She agreed to that arrangement, but there was nothing in the arrangement that excluded watching the evening news.

Dinner is ready, but once again Henry is late. She switches on the evening news, thinking, *I'll just watch for a while and turn it off when I hear him stomp the snow off his boots on the front porch. What he doesn't know won't hurt him.*

A handsome anchorman named Roger Newman smiles as he introduces investigative reporter Billie Simmons. Ms. Simmons is the Channel 10 reporter following the exploits of a mass murderer the police refer to as the Butcher.

The Butcher is credited with committing thirteen murders in the last six months. His M.O. is to stalk and murder young women, dismember their bodies, place the body parts in plastic bags and spread them around for the police to locate. The police have received hundreds of calls regarding the Butcher on their crime line but none of the tips have panned out. They're under a lot of pressure from City Hall and the citizens to make an arrest, because every day the Butcher continues to roam free is another day young women in the city live in fear.

The flashing lights and police activity in the background behind Ms. Simmons are an indication that the Butcher has struck again.

Ms. Simmons puts on her serious face as she prepares to speak. "Earlier today, two joggers discovered the gruesome remains of a body in Munsey Park. The runners were startled when they noticed several large rats running in and out of a waste receptacle. Upon closer inspection they discovered that the rats were gnawing on what appeared to be a human hand, so they immediately contacted the police."

Oh my God, thinks Andrea, *that's so gross. Not something I wanted to hear just before dinner.*

"After cordoning off the crime scene, police searched the area and discovered nine other plastic bags containing the body parts of what they believe to be a single victim. The police are still at the scene collecting evidence and have yet to comment on this grisly murder."

"Billie," the anchorman says, "have the police or one of the joggers who discovered the crime scene mentioned if the body parts were those of a male or female?"

"No," replies Billie with a perturbed look. "The police have not made a statement, and witnesses are still being questioned."

"If you had to speculate," says Roger, "and I hate to ask you to do this, but our viewers want to know. Would you say that this crime scene is consistent with other crime scenes attributed to the Butcher?"

Billie replies, "I don't think it would be appropriate for me to speculate, but the crime scene and the method of disposing the body are certainly consistent with the Butcher's previous murders."

"As far as you know, have all the body parts been recovered?"

Billie looks into the camera with an expression that says, *Have you listened to a single word I've said?*

"Ah, the police have not made any formal announcement, so there's no way to verify the answer to your question."

"So, you suspect that this is indeed the work of the Butcher."

"My gut feeling says yes, but until we hear from the police, there's no way we can rule out a possible copycat murder."

"Hmm, a copycat murder? How intriguing," says Roger, almost purring at the thought. "What about the rumors flying around that there may be cannibalism involved?"

"Again, the accusation of cannibalism is pure speculation. However, my inside sources inform me that the police have not recovered all of the body parts from previous Butcher crime scenes."

"Are you implying that The Butcher is keeping a souvenir of each victim?" he says, raising an eyebrow.

"I'll leave that for our viewers to decide," Billie says with a cynical smile, "I'll just stick with the facts."

"Thanks, Billie. That was an intriguing report. Please keep us posted when new information is available."

"This is Billie Simmons reporting from Munsey Park. Back to you…"

As the camera cuts to Roger in the studio, Andrea can hear Billie say, "Asshole."

Wow! That was truly awful reporting, thinks Andrea. *Maybe Henry's right. I need to stop watching this crap before it rots my brain. If Henry were here, he'd give me a lecture on how TV news is just sensationalized bullshit.*

"In a related story," the anchorman says, "police are searching for the man caught on video at a local convenience store earlier today. The police received an anonymous tip about this individual in relation to the Butcher murder case. If anyone recognizes this man and knows his whereabouts, please contact the police immediately."

Andrea clasps both hands over her mouth as she stares at the grainy video and recognizes her husband, Henry.

"Oh my God, oh my God, he promised me he would stop," she says, stomping her feet. "Damn you, Henry, you promised."

She hears boots stomping on the front porch and quickly turns off the TV. He walks in and says, "Hi, babe, sorry I'm late. The buses were running slow tonight. Looks like another snowstorm's coming."

She gives him a look that tells him clearly that something's wrong. He looks down at his smock and then folds his arms across his chest, trying to hide all the bloodstains.

"Honey, I know you hate when I come home wearing my dirty smock, but I had no choice. I spilled coffee all over my good shirt this morning and thought I'd look like a total slob wearing it on the bus in that condition."

"And you thought this would be better?" she says, pointing at his bloody work smock.

"No, but I gotta admit that it got lots of interesting looks on the bus," he says, laughing out loud.

He's told her about the looks on people's faces when they see him get on the bus with blood all over his smock. It usually takes them a few minutes before they notice the business logo on his left breast pocket, which reads *Dan's House of Meat – Established in 1955.* Then they smile in relief and turn away in disgust.

"You've got the strangest sense of humor, Henry Foster, but that's not what I'm mad about and you damn well know it."

"Oh, come on, babe. You knew when you married me that I was in the meat business and that butchers work strange hours. I can't help it that the delivery truck was late today. You know I have to stay until everything's been unloaded and stored in the freezer," he says, pleading his case.

Henry is from a family of butchers and Dan's House of Meat has been the family business for 60 years.

Started by his grandfather Daniel back in the fifties, the shop has always been known for its quality meats, reasonable prices and wonderful 'slice to order' services.

When Grandpa Daniel died, he passed the shop on to his son Finley, Henry's father. Fin Foster, like his old man, was known as a good and honest butcher and taught his son Henry everything he knew about the business.

When Fin passed away last year, Henry took over the shop. He's the third generation of Fosters running the business. It's been a huge responsibility for Henry, trying to keep the family business thriving and living up to his father's reputation in the community.

Andrea has heard the story a hundred times: there was never any doubt that Henry would be a butcher. As a child he was always in the shop helping his father and grandfather. By the time he was a teenager he'd developed a talent for being a fast and precise carver of meats. He loved the smell of raw meat and the feel of cold steel in his hands. Working in the shop makes him happy and provides a good living. The only down sides to the business are the long, late working hours and the messy conditions.

"I'm sorry I'm late, but it couldn't be helped."

"You're a liar, Henry Foster. I keep telling you, you need to get help."

"Andrea, you know I can't afford to hire more help at the shop," he replies frustrated.

"That's not what I'm talking about, and you know it. You told me you would stop. You said you could handle it without seeking professional help. You promised me after the last incident that it would be your last time, but today you did it again."

"I have no idea what you're talking about, Andrea," he says with a confused and nervous look.

"How can I trust you if you refuse to acknowledge you have a problem? Maybe you don't care about me or even yourself, but I can't continue to let you hurt people and run around like a maniac."

"Oh, dear God, I must be tired," he says, running his fingers through his hair, "because I have no earthly idea what you're babbling on about."

"Let me smell your breath."

"What?"

"You heard me. Let me smell your breath." She smells his breath and says, "Just as I suspected… and a video I saw on the news just confirmed."

"What video? I thought I told you not to watch the damn news."

"You've been drinking again, haven't you?" she asks. Then, not waiting for a response, she says sharply, "Don't bother pretending otherwise, because I saw you in that video from Melnick's convenience store, buying a six-pack."

"What the hell? Is the news day so slow that they've got nothing better to do than run videos of Melnick's customers?"

"Everything is a joke to you, isn't it? Keep this up and you'll end up dead or in prison," she says with venom in her voice.

"Okay, okay, guilty as charged, but why the hell was I on the news?"

"You were on the news because the guy in line ahead of you at Melnick's is wanted for questioning by the police in regard to the Butcher case."

"Do they think he's the Butcher?"

"I have no idea what they think," she says, frustrated, "and I don't care."

"Wow, I wonder if they knew there were two butchers in the same line?" he says with a straight face and then begins giggling.

Andrea tries not to smile, but the sound of Henry's laughter makes it difficult. "I married an insane person," she says in frustration.

"Come on, babe, you gotta admit that was pretty darn funny."

"Yes, maybe, but your continued drinking isn't. Have you forgotten what the judge said to you the last time he suspended your license? Don't you want to drive again? Keep this up and you'll be riding the bus the rest of your life."

"Of course, I remember what he said," he replies in a serious tone. "What do you want me to say? I screwed up. Are you happy now?"

"No, I want you to keep your promise to stop drinking."

"Okay, I promise it won't happen again. I swear to God and on my father's grave, it will not happen again."

"If you lie to me again, Henry Foster, I swear to God and on my mother's grave that I will leave you. I'm dead serious. I won't live with a man who thinks it's alright to lie to his wife. If you carry on like this, I'll be a widow before I'm forty. I refuse to let that happen."

"Understood," he says solemnly. "Now can I please go downstairs and wash up for dinner?"

"Fine," she says with a look of relief. "I made your favorite pot roast and I need my master carver to slice it up."

"*Mon plaisir, madame,*" he says in a mock French accent as he kisses her hand and the side of her neck. "I shall return *bientôt.*"

"Don't forget to feed your dogs before you come back upstairs."

"Will do, honey bear."

That was close, he thinks as he heads down the stairs to the basement and locks the door behind him. He can't believe his rotten luck, getting caught on camera with the damn beer. If she only knew the truth, she would have left him long ago. He decides to be more careful and selective about where he does business.

He turns on the water in the shower as he strips off his soiled work clothes. He tosses the clothes toward the washing machine, then puts on his robe and steps outside into the back yard through the basement entrance. He carries some scraps of meat he brought home for his canine girls, who are howling in anticipation.

"Enjoy, my sweet ladies. There's much more where this came from," he says, smiling.

Back inside, he disrobes and is about to step into the shower when he remembers there's something important, he forgot to do. Naked, he walks to the storage cabinet, unlocks the combination lock, pulls out a large Mason jar and places it on his work bench. He feels aroused as he rifles through his dirty clothes and pulls out something sealed in a plastic bag.

He drops the object into the fluid-filled Mason jar and says, "Girls, say hello to our new friend Debra," as the pretty blue eye joins the eyeballs from his previous victims.

As he seals the jar and places it back in the cabinet, he thinks, *I'm taking a big chance, storing you girls in this house, but I can't help myself. I need my babies close at hand so I can come down here after Andrea's asleep and play with my girls.*

"See you later, pretty ladies," he says, then blows a kiss, shuts the cabinet door, and twirls the combination lock closed.

Climbing into the shower, he feels the warm water striking his skin and thinks that like John the Baptist baptizing Jesus in the Jordan River, his sins are being forgiven.

Blame it on the Weather

2019 Finalist in Royal Palm Literary Competition
(Short Story Genre)

I watch as snowflakes land gently on my windshield and quickly melt away. It's a bitter, cold morning and I'm sitting in the back corner of the parking lot, with a bottle of Jack Daniels in my hand and the car heater running at full capacity.

The burning sensation of the whiskey sliding down my throat feels good, but nothing can extinguish the chilling feeling of this long-awaited day. I pull down the sun visor to shield my eyes from the bright morning sun as it crests over the empty field across from the station. A photograph of my daughter stares back at me on the dashboard.

I take a deep breath as I realize how quickly my heart is filled with anger and sadness. I feel moisture building in the corner of my eyes, but I dash it away using the sleeve of my camouflage jacket.

"Cut this shit out right now, Blake!" I growl between my teeth as I drop my head against the steering wheel"

"There's no time for this. Not this morning, not today."

I slowly raise my head, stare at her photograph and think, *This will all be over soon, sweetheart. I just want to stop hurting.*

I snatch the photograph from the dashboard, place it against my lips, kiss it and rest it against the steering wheel.

"I love you, little girl, and I miss you every day."

I took this photograph on Christmas day, a year ago—I remember it as if it were yesterday. Sherrie had just turned eight in November and there she was holding up the new pair of figure skates that Santa had brought her for Christmas. The smile on her face radiates happiness and her eyes beam with excitement, capturing the beauty of the moment.

Sherrie was crazy about ice skating. From the minute she hit the rink at the age of three, she loved everything about it. Anyone who saw her skate said she was a natural. It wasn't long before my wife and I were approached by several coaches at the local arena, asking if we were interested in enrolling her in figure skating classes.

By the time she was seven, she was an excellent skater and would make a point of telling anyone who asked that she was going to be a professional figure skater when she grew up. She had Disney on Ice posters covering every wall of her bedroom. It was her dream to travel around the country with the show and skate in all the big arenas with Elsa, Anna, and Moana.

I pull the photograph against my chest and hold it tightly as I wait for another wave of emotions to subside. I breathe out, then take another swig from the bottle.

It's amazing how everything you love can be taken from you in the blink of an eye. One day you're happy and full of life and the next you're divorced, unemployed and broke.

In my prayers I've often asked God, *Why me? What did I do to deserve this?*

I've been waiting patiently for an answer, but either God's not listening, or he doesn't care. Either way I'm done waiting.

I sip another mouthful of whiskey from the bottle, and then remind myself to take it slow. It's been years since I've craved a cigarette, but I could kill for one right about now. I promised Sherrie I would stop smoking and three years ago I did. As much as I crave a smoke right now, I would never break my promise, not now, not ever.

I rub my tired, blood-shot eyes and think about all the sleepless nights I've endured over the past year. The face in the mirror staring back at me looks like a complete stranger, the sad remains of a once proud and happy father and husband. I'm not sure I'll ever be the man I once was, but today will be a step in taking my life back.

My thoughts are distracted by the sound of a loud noise coming from the tail pipes of an all too familiar red Ford Mustang. I watch the driver pull the vehicle into his designated parking space and switch off the engine, but he doesn't leave the driver's seat. He's on his cell phone, and from the way he's flailing his arms in the air he appears to be having a full-blown argument with someone on the other end of the call.

I feel a smile building in the corners of my mouth, knowing that I'm more than likely the cause of his animated conversation. I've been following him around for days and I discovered that the scumbag's been cheating on his wife. Under the circumstances I thought it only fair that I give his wife a heads up about his sexual indiscretions. The poor slob's already beginning his day on the wrong foot and now it's about to get much worse.

I watch him rip the cell phone from its stand, open the driver side door and jump out of the car. I can hear his voice speaking into the phone, but I can't make out what he's saying. By the look on his face, he doesn't appear to be enjoying the conversation. He opens the rear door on the driver's side, pulls out a briefcase, and then slams the door shut.

I slip the bottle of whiskey into the side pocket of my jacket, step out of my vehicle, and walk quickly toward him. He now has his back to me and is walking toward the building, too busy screaming into the cell phone to see or hear me sneak up behind him.

"I told you, Viv, I was at Andy's place last night! Why the hell don't you believe me! You know Thursday's poker night. I had a few too many, alright! I just passed out on his sofa. I woke up this morning with a blanket over me and a splitting headache."

He listens to the voice on the other end, then says, "I planned on calling you, but I told you I passed out. What part of that don't you understand?"

He listens once more and shakes his head. "And you believe some asshole who calls you in the middle of the night, spreading lies about me. Nice, Viv. Really nice. You believe a total stranger rather than your own husband!"

He pauses again, listening, then replies, "It was two in the goddamn morning when Harry picked up the phone. He was drunk and probably half asleep, that's why he told you I wasn't there. That's all there is to it. I was sleeping on the sofa; I'm not cheating on you, so stop being so damn paranoid."

There's apparently more talk from the other end, then I hear him say, "We'll talk about this later; I need to wash up, change my clothes and get to work."

He slides the cell phone into his right pants pocket and mutters to himself, "Jesus, like I really need to hear this shit right now!"

"Having a bad day, Mr. Clement?" I ask as I shove the barrel of my pistol into the small of his back. "Can I call you Jimmy?"

"What the fu-...!" He attempts to turn and face me.

"Now, now—I suggest you don't do that."

"What the hell is going on?" he asks in a shaky voice, then raises both arms above his head.

"Put your damn arms down or I'll shoot you right here and now."

In a panic he drops his arms. He loses control of his briefcase, and it crashes to the ground.

"Pick it up," I tell him. "If you make another move like that, I will hurt you. Do you understand?"

He nods his head and retrieves the bag without turning toward me.

In a trembling voice he asks, "Is this a robbery? Because if it is, I have a hundred and twenty dollars in my pocket and some credit cards in my wallet. The cards are pretty much maxed out, so they won't do you much good but take the cash and my car keys. Take whatever you want, just don't hurt me."

"I don't want your damn money."

"Then what do you want?"

"I want you to suffer."

"Did my wife send you?"

He can't see the smile on my face as I reply, "No, but I'm sure she appreciated my phone call last night."

"You're the guy who called her? Why would you do that?"

"I hope that piece of ass you were doing last night was worth the hefty divorce settlement coming your way?"

"Were you following me?"

"What do you think?"

"My wife won't leave me. She always believes what I tell her." He says in a smug tone.

"I guess we'll put your theory to the test when your wife gets the photographs, I sent her in an email this morning."

"You're bluffing!"

I laugh out loud. "Am I?"

"You goddamn bastard! What the hell do you want from me?"

"I want you to confess the truth and to take responsibility for your actions."

"What are you, some self-righteous asshole vigilante who defends women who've been wronged? Is that it?"

"Feeling brave, are you, Jimmy Boy?" I ask in a playful tone. "What makes you think this is about your wife?"

"Then I don't understand. What is it you want? Why are you doing this?"

"So many questions and so few answers."

"How can I give you what you want if I don't know what it is?" he says with a pleading tone in his voice.

I poke the gun into his back. "I want you to go inside the TV station and take me to your dressing room, office or wherever you go to get ready for your show."

"Not until you tell me why."

The nerve of this little shit! The guy has more balls than I thought. I turn my gun and strike him between the shoulders with the butt. He cries out in pain and his knees buckle.

"Alright, we'll play it your way. Get the hell up and start walking toward the wooded area."

"Why?" he asks, too frightened to turn around and look at me.

"No more questions. If you won't take me inside, then I don't need you anymore."

He jumps up and pleads. "No! No! I'll do what you say."

"No more questions until we are safely inside. Please understand that I'll be more than happy to put a bullet in your spine if you try to run or cause a disturbance. Don't piss me off again, Jimmy. I have little to live for and nothing to lose."

"If what you're saying is true then how do I know you won't kill me even if I do everything you ask of me?"

"That's the thing, Jimmy, you don't," I reply angrily. "What part of 'no more questions' did you not understand?" I ask, striking him in the shoulder one more time and letting out a sinister laugh.

We begin walking toward the building entrance and I hear him say under his breath, "Crazy motherfu-...!" He breaks off, and I decide to let it slide.

We enter the Tri-County News Channel 4 building through the front doors and walk toward the security desk where a guard sits with his feet up on the counter, flipping through a copy of HGTV Magazine. He drops his feet to the floor and stands before we reach the counter.

Clement looks at the security guard and says, "Good morning, Bruce."

The guard smiles and says, "Morning, Mr. Clements. It's Roger, remember?"

I jam the gun into Clement's ribs and hear him say, "Ouch."

The guard looks at me, then back at Clement.

Clement says, "Sorry Roger. I was listening to Springsteen in the car, and I had Bruce on my mind. Honest mistake."

"No problem, Mr. Clement. Who's the gentleman with you?"

Clement turns his head toward me and looks at me for the first time, but I can see by the expression on his face that he has no idea who I am.

"Ahhh. This is my cousin, umm, Al-Albert. I invited him to watch this morning's broadcast."

Roger smiles, extends his hand and says, "Nice to meet you, Albert."

I nod at him, but I don't reciprocate, so he pulls his hand back. He places a pen and clipboard on the counter, points at it and says, "Please sign in," then hands me a visitor's badge. "You need to wear this badge at all times while you're in the studio, and make sure you sign out and return it when you leave."

Shielded from Roger's view by Clements body, I quickly shift the gun to my left hand, I pick up the pen, sign on the clipboard and say, "No problem, Rog. You don't mind if I call you Rog, do you?"

He shrugs his shoulders, sits down, picks up the magazine and goes back to reading, without bothering to glance at the bogus name I signed on the clipboard: Albert Capone.

Poor dimwitted Roger, he's going to have a lot of explaining to do before this day is over, I think, as we walk past the security desk down the well-lit hallway.

"Try that stunt again and you're dead," I growl at Clement. "Understand!"

I hear Clement swallow hard before saying, "Understood."

I shake my head, then roll my eyes. "The security in this place is an absolute joke."

Clement answers without looking back, "That idiot is the station manager's nephew. Not the sharpest tool in the shed."

"Under the circumstances, it's nice to hear that you haven't lost your sense of humor, Jimmy."

"Don't let my calm exterior fool you. I'm scared shitless, Mister. I'm not the hero type, but if I could take that gun from you I would in a heartbeat."

I place my hand on his shoulder and press the gun into the center of his spine, "So why don't you?"

"Because I think you're crazy enough to shoot me and anyone who attempts to help me. I won't take that chance. I won't have that on my conscience."

"Smart, Jimmy Boy, very smart indeed," I say, tapping the side of his head with the back of my hand.

"This is my office," he says as we arrive in front of a door bearing his name.

I reach for the doorknob, turn it and find it locked. He reaches into his pocket.

"Easy, Jimmy. The key better be the only thing you're reaching for."

He holds his hand up in the air, dangles a set of keys and gives me a look that says, *How stupid do you think I am?*

"Good boy," I say in a patronizing tone of voice. "I'd hate to have to turn you in for breaking and entering."

He gives me a puzzled look, then throws the keys on his desk and plops down into his chair.

"Hands on the desk," I say.

He obeys, then asks, "Now what? You still haven't told me what the hell this is about."

I lock the door behind us and sit down in the chair across from him, still pointing the gun at him.

"How long have you been a TV weatherman, Jimmy?"

"I'll have you know that I'm not just a TV weatherman, I'm a meteorologist, have been for twelve years. Why?"

"Twelve years and you still don't know shit about weather forecasting."

I see an irritated look flash across his face and wait for his defensive response.

"What do you know about weather?" he replies, crossing his arms in defiance. "I'll have you know that I've won several awards for my work as a weather... I mean meteorologist. Viewers rely on my forecasts every day. I've been voted best forecaster in the Tri-County area for the last five years. Is this what this is all about? You think I'm a lousy forecaster?"

I place the gun on my lap and clap my hands together in mock applause. "Well bravo, Jimmy Boy. Is that what you want to hear?"

"Go ahead and mock me, but I know I'm good at what I do."

"All those bullshit accolades from your peers don't disguise the truth."

"And what truth is that?"

"The fact that your forecasts are dead wrong half of the time."

His face turns a deep shade of red, "That's not true! Who told you that?"

"I don't need anyone to tell me that, all I had to do was do the math."

"What math?"

"I've been tracking your forecasts for the last 365 days, and guess what? You've been wrong fifty percent of the time. That's the same probability rate as flipping a coin 365 times and getting a head. Face it, Jimmy, you're just a big fraud."

"Even if what you say is true, though I don't believe it... what's it to you? Why do you give a shit if I'm right or wrong half the time? This is America, why don't you just turn the channel? There are plenty of other weather forecasters you can watch. What do you want from me, an apology? Is that what this is about?"

"Did you ever think that maybe, just maybe, what you do has an effect on people's lives?"

"So what? It's just the weather! If I'm wrong, you can just look out your window and grab a sweater or umbrella. Jesus, get a life!"

"Get a life!" I repeat as I jump to my feet, lunge across the desk, and grab him by the throat.

He makes a gagging sound, and his eyes start from his head.

"I had a life, you little prick, but you and your goddamn forecast took it away from me! You took away the two best things in my life and now I'm here to hold you accountable."

I can see by the fearful look in his eyes that Jimmy has no idea where I'm going with this, nor what I might be capable of. I release his throat, and watch him slump back in his chair, his breath rasping, and massage his throat.

He waves his hands in front of me and pleads, "Listen, Mister, I have no beef with you. Whatever you think I've done, whatever aggravation I may have caused you… I'm truly sorry."

"Your show of remorse is touching, but it's not enough. If you want me to spare your life and those of your colleagues, I suggest that you listen carefully and do everything I tell you."

He gives me a mortified look and for a moment I think he's going to break down and cry, but he sits back instead and buries his face in his hands.

"Just tell me what you want. I'll do whatever you say, just don't do anything stupid."

The tone in his voice seems filled with sincerity. It must have finally dawned on him that he has no choice but to do what I ask him to do.

"Calm down, Jimmy," I say as I pull the bottle of Jack Daniels out of my coat pocket. I remove the bottle cap, take a swig and place it on the desk in front of him.

"You look like you need a drink."

"No thanks."

"Suit yourself," I reply, taking the bottle back. I pull a folded sheet of paper out of my pocket and hand it to him.

"What's this?" he asks with a confused look on his face.

"I want you to read this on air this morning."

He takes the note from me and begins reading it to himself. He stops, looks up at me and says, "I can't say this on air. It will ruin me."

"That's the point, Jimmy Boy. I want you to suffer like I've suffered over the past year. I want you to feel what it's like to lose everything that's near and dear to you."

"But, but, this is insane. I can't say this on live television!"

"You can and you will."

"You don't really believe this! Do you?"

"Is that a rhetorical question?" I let out a loud chuckle. "Of course, I believe it. Do you think I'd go to all this trouble if I didn't?"

"You're not thinking straight. Your personal tragedy has nothing to do with me."

I take another swig from the bottle and give him a menacing look.

He stares at the bottle in my hand and then up at me. "You like to drink, don't you?"

"So, what's it to you?"

"Just wondering if you were sober on the day of the accident."

I slam the bottle on the desk, lunge forward and grab his throat again.

"You two-bit amateur butt wipe, I don't like what your implying! Do you think I'd drive drunk with my daughter in the car? Yes, I may have had a couple of drinks, but it takes a lot to get me drunk. I don't give a damn what the police report said, I wasn't fucking drunk and I'm goddamn sick and tired of people telling me I'm wrong about this."

I feel him try to swallow and he looks like he's going to faint, so I ease my grip on his throat and shove him back into his chair. He rubs his throat and has a coughing fit.

"You will read that damn note word for word, Jimmy. If you leave anything out or lose your nerve, I will kill you on live television."

"But... you'll never get away with this. After I've read your note, you'll be arrested and thrown in jail."

"Hollow threats, my friend. Do you think I don't know that? The only question is, are you going to do the right thing, or will this have to end in a bloody mess?"

Jimmy's shoulders slump forward as I look at him read and reread the note.

I smile and watch closely for his reaction to my next question.

"By the way, did you have a good time with my ex-wife last night? She can be quite the ball of fire when she wants to be."

His eyes grow large and bright, like high beams on a dark night. He tries to respond, but his throat is completely dry. He grabs the bottle of Jack Daniels and takes a long pull, then puts it down, picks it up again and takes another pull.

His voice returns and he says, "You're going to kill me. Aren't you?"

We both hear a knock at the door and a voice say, "You're on in five, Mister Clement."

I point the gun at him and whisper, "Answer her. Damn it."

"Thanks Annette. I'm on my way."

He attempts to stand up but is so upset that he loses his balance and almost drops the bottle, before sitting back down.

I take the bottle away and throw him a reassuring smile, "You can do it, Jimmy. I have complete faith in you," I wink at him.

He tosses a look of bewilderment in my direction and says, "You're insane. You're certifiably nuts."

"Yup. And I'm holding the gun."

I hear him whisper, "Shit. I'm screwed!"

I stand up, walk toward the door and say, "It's show time, Jimmy!" Then I adjust my visitor's badge to make sure it's clearly visible and unlock the office door.

I raise my left arm and gesture toward the open door. "After you, Mr. Clement."

As he attempts to walk past me, I grab his arm and spin him around.

"Haven't you forgotten something?"

I see the confused look as he asks, "What?"

"You left the goddamn note on the desk, asshole. You need to focus if you want this to end well!"

He retrieves the note, looks me in the eye and says, "Ends well for who?" as we walk slowly toward the studio set.

"When you get up there, don't try anything funny. I'll be watching your every move from the sideline. If you try to run or warn anyone, I'll put a bullet in you. Do you understand me?"

He swallows, licks his lips to relieve the dryness, and nods in defeat.

"Have fun out there. This performance will probably get you the highest ratings of your entire career," I say, grinning from ear to ear.

I watch him fidget as he waits for his cue. The blonde anchorwoman finally introduces him.

"And now here's Jim Clement with a look at our local weather. Is it ever going to stop snowing around here, Jim?"

The camera pans toward Jimmy standing in front of the green screen that is going to have the weather map projected onto it. He stares into the camera, but he doesn't speak.

The blonde newswoman glances at her co-anchor who says, "I think you caught Jim by surprise, Vilma. I believe it's the first time he's ever been speechless."

Everyone on the set lets out an uncomfortable laugh which seems to snap Clement out of his trance.

He puts on a forced smile and says, "Thank you, Vilma. To answer your question, no, the snow's not going to stop anytime soon."

I hear everyone at the anchor desk let out a sigh of relief.

Clement looks over at me and I give him an angry look. The bastard looks like he might chicken out, so I mouth the words, *Read the damn note*!

To my surprise he begins reading.

"Dear Viewers, I have a confession to make. I, James Clement, am a fraud."

I hear whispers coming from the anchor desk and a voice saying, "What's going on?"

To his credit Clement continues reading. "I honestly have no idea what the weather is going to be one hour, one day or one week from today. My credentials as a meteorologist don't make me any more capable of predicting the weather, then a phony fortuneteller has the capability of telling you what will happen to you in the future. If you check my forecasting record, you'll notice that I'm wrong fifty percent of the time. I've always believed in the saying *'no harm no foul'*; after all, if I predict the weather incorrectly what possible harm can come from that?"

Clement wipes away the bead of sweat from his forehead and continues.

"Unfortunately, all actions have consequences, even my less-than-stellar forecasting skills. A year ago, on this very day, my incorrect weather forecast resulted in the death of eight–year-old future figure skater Sherrie Marie Thomas."

He stops and I notice a tear run down his cheek. I think, *Quite the performance, Jimmy Boy.*

"Sherrie and her father were on their way home from a performance of Disney on Ice when a heavy snowstorm hit. I had predicted that the storm wouldn't affect the area until the following day—but once again I was wrong, dead wrong. Their car hit a hidden patch of black ice, spun out of control, and flew off an embankment into a snow-covered retention pond. Little Sherrie was pronounced dead at the scene of the accident." He places a hand over his mouth and looks like he may break down and cry.

He regains his composure and continues, "I am deeply saddened by what happened and I take full responsibility for my involvement in the death of this child."

Clement looks at me and for a moment I'm moved by the genuine appearance of pain and sincerity on his face. His mouth is distorted, there are tears running down his cheeks and his body begins to shake and to rock, back and forth. He looks like he's about to break into convulsions, when suddenly I hear a long, loud, unmistakable sound.

Purr ruff!!

I hear a roar from the sidelines. "Cut! Cut! Who's the son of a bitch who farted?" The director comes stomping into the set, his face red with irritation.

Clement, or rather, Josh Parker, veteran actor of Silver Screen Studios, is falling on both knees, unable to contain himself. He hits the floor, rolls on his back, and roars out in uncontrollable laughter.

The director throws his headset at him and screams, "Parker, you dumb shit. Was that you?"

Parker gains his composure long enough to nod his head and wheeze out between bursts of laughter, "Who wrote this awful script? This is the worse pile of crap I've ever read."

Now everyone in the studio is laughing hysterically.

I figure it's time to have some fun, so I walk across the set to where Parker is lying, point my weapon at him and say, "You son of a bitch, after everything you've done to ruin my life, that was the most unremorseful-sounding fart I've ever heard."

Parker's eyes grow large, and I see the playful expression on his tearful face. He raises his arms in a mock gesture and says, "You promised nothing would happen if I read your stupid note. You promised me."

"Well, I lied," I say, then pull the trigger and watch a stream of grape juice splatter across his face and clothes.

He jumps up and begins chasing me around the set, as everyone bursts into laughter once again.

In the corner of my eye, I see the director smiling and shaking his head.

He stands with his hands on his hips and says, "Okay. Okay! Boys will be boys. Let's all take an early lunch break. Everyone be back here in one hour, especially you two!" He points directly at me and Josh.

Then he turns back toward the set. "Where the hell's that bottle of Jack Daniels?"

True Confession

He was thirteen years old when he heard the call.

All his friends and even his parents were certain that the phase would pass once he attended college and discovered girls. It was a big shock to them when during his first semester he dropped out of college and joined the seminary.

His mother lamented, "What boy really knows what he wants to be at the age of eighteen?"

His parents were bewildered by his decision. His father would often joke that this just proved that the boy took after his wife's side of the family because his family was filled with lushes, scoundrels, and thieves.

Marco's parents had been raised Catholic but didn't practice their faith on a regular basis. Christmas, Easter and the occasional baptism, wedding or funeral were the extent of their involvement in the church. When asked about his religious convictions, his father would refer to himself as a 'Cafeteria Catholic', someone who chose what he wanted to believe and rejected what he didn't.

Marco attended Catholic school because that was where good Italian parents sent their children. The boy needed to learn right from wrong, and who else but the priests and nuns could put the fear of God in his soul.

Marco was a remarkably good student, but to his parents' dismay the classes he excelled in were all religious study classes. He loved attending catechism instruction and Bible study classes, even when attendance was not mandatory. He volunteered to be an altar boy as soon as he was old enough to do so and took his responsibility very seriously. So seriously that in times of stress he would often throw up before mass in fear of making a mistake in front of his peers.

His parents worried about him because he was too young to place so much pressure on himself. Being such poor Catholics, they couldn't blame themselves for Marco's obsession with the faith, so they accused the nuns of forcing their son in a direction they did not approve of and threatened to remove the boy from Catholic school.

When Marco discovered what they were planning, he ran away and disappeared for two days. As it turned out, he hadn't really run away, but was hiding out at his grandmother's house. He refused to go home. His parents were frantic, thinking the boy had been kidnapped or, God forbid, murdered. The day they filed a missing person report, he showed up on their doorstep with Nonna. A hideous argument ensued when Nonna attempted to explain the situation.

Marco's father went ballistic, going as far as calling his mother-in-law *pazza* (crazy) and threatening to have her institutionalized or arrested for kidnapping. Fortunately, cooler heads prevailed, and Marco's parents consented to have him complete his primary education in Catholic school.

Unknown to his parents, Nonna Maria was his biggest supporter and religious instigator. She was thrilled with the thought of her grandson becoming a priest. She would often say, "This family could do a lot worse than having a priest in the fold."

He enjoyed hanging out with his Nonna, so he visited her as often as he could. She loved to tell him stories about Jesus, the

Apostles, Jonah and the Whale, Moses, and the parting of the Red Sea and about all the saints who had sacrificed their lives to do God's work. She would ask Marco what he wanted to be when he grew up, and Marco would reply, "A saint. I want to be a saint in God's army."

"That's *mio bambino*," she'd say. "And how do you become a saint?"

"By joining the priesthood, spreading God's word, helping the less fortunate and defending my beliefs, no matter what."

"*Bravo, caro mio.* You're going to make your Nonna very proud someday."

Proud, indeed, he thinks as he sits before a nearly empty sanctuary in St. Anne's Church in crime-riddled Belleview parish. All those years of study and sacrifice at the seminary didn't prepare him for the evil he's witnessed over the last five years, since he became a priest. He was so certain that he was ready to tackle any problem set before him that he begged the bishop to assign him to the worst parish in the city.

What a fool I was, he thinks. *How arrogant of me to believe that I could make a difference to these drug-peddling children, murderers, rapists, alcoholics, prostitutes, human traffickers, and whatever other form of evil walks around this parish.*

A soldier of God, he thinks as a smile crosses his face. *They never told me that the battle would be so overwhelming and the victories so few.*

He waits as the collection plate is brought forward and placed before the altar. A quick glance tells him that this morning's collection probably amounts to fifty dollars, two beer caps, one hypodermic needle and five cigarette butts. Most of the poor slobs attending mass are simply trying to avoid the bitter cold and snow that rages outside; they aren't here to share in the feast of communion or listen to the word of God.

For many of these people, God is just a concept, a fairy tale, a lie to keep them docile in their poverty. Eternal life after death and heaven mean little to the poor and the starving; it's all about the here and now, and *what can the church do to help me?* A life of misery in return for a future of happiness in God's everlasting kingdom is a tough pill to swallow when your children are crying and hungry.

As bad as the daily mass service appears to Father Marco, it doesn't compare to the hodge-podge of unruly characters who attend confession on Wednesday nights. Yes, there are a few honest, thoughtful souls who are truly sorry for their sins and ask God for forgiveness, but most of the flock asks for forgiveness, yet feels no remorse for their sins. These are the ones who frustrate him the most, those who walk out of his confessional and back to a life of crime.

He feels a light tug on his sleeve and stares at the face of Johnny Bello, the altar boy, reminding him that he is once again lost in his thoughts and needs to concentrate on the mass. He smiles, pats the boy on the head and completes the 6 a.m. mass.

Back in the vestry after mass, Johnny approaches Father Marco and asks if everything is okay.

"Yes, son, I'm just fine. Thank you for bringing me back to reality so I could complete the service," he says with a smile.

"What were you thinking about, Father? Was God speaking to you during mass?"

Poor naïve boy. Sometimes Father Marco wishes he could tell him the truth, but sooner or later the boy will find out on his own.

"Johnny, you ask too many questions," he replies with a laugh.

Johnny smiles back, and it's clear that he's happy to hear Father Marco laugh.

"Father, when you heard the call, was it the voice of God?"

"What call are you referring to, my son?" he asks.

"The call to become a priest… was it the voice of God?"

Father Marco bursts out laughing and says, "Not unless my Nonna was pretending to be the voice of our Lord."

Johnny gives him a confused look and Father Marco feels guilty for his flippant remark. He knows that the boy is serious about becoming a priest and it isn't fair of him to pass on his jaded view of the priesthood to someone so young.

"No, it wasn't the voice of God I heard," he says truthfully. "It was just a feeling in my heart that told me it was the right path for me. I know that some say God speaks to them, but that was not my experience. Does that make sense, Johnny?"

"Yes, Father. Thank you for telling me. I was getting concerned because God hasn't spoken to me, but now I know not to worry," the boy says with a smile.

"Will I see you tonight?"

"Yes, Father. Seven o'clock sharp."

"Good boy. We'll pray together."

Johnny lives across the street from the church and comes over every evening. He sits in the front pew, kneels in prayer, and waits for God's call. Father Marco has great respect for the boy. He envies the pure devotion the child has towards God and the church. It reminds him of someone he once knew, someone who lost his way long ago.

* * *

It's Wednesday morning and the housekeeper Mrs. Sardy is preparing omelets for breakfast as Father Marco walks into the kitchen. He sits as she serves him the best omelet in town. A few moments later Monsignor Bryan walks in and grabs a cup of coffee. Mrs. Sardy asks him if he wants breakfast, but he informs her that he's meeting his sister at Starbucks and they're going to Denny's for brunch.

"Say hello to Margret," says Father Marco. "Give her my regards. I hope the two of you enjoy your time together."

"I will, Father, and thanks again for taking my rotation at confession tonight. I guess I'll owe you one," Monsignor Bryan says with a smile.

"Nonsense. I seem to recall you bailing me out a time or two since I've been at this parish."

"Ah – glad to know you're keeping track," Monsignor Bryan says as he heads for the door.

The man has been Monsignor of this church for twenty-six years and Father Marco has no idea how he's done it without going completely insane. He is one of those old-time priests who don't allow anything to get to them; not one word of despair or negativity has ever escaped from his lips. Although Father Marco envies the man's dedication to the church, he also knows that he could never emulate him.

When your face has been slapped by the forces of evil, it's not always easy or advisable to turn the other cheek. Sometimes a Soldier of God needs to take matters into his own hands and do what he believes is right. Father Marco is that soldier and he takes his role in God's army seriously. Some might call it vigilantism, but he calls it justice, and he's sure that he has God's approval and more importantly, God's forgiveness.

April Patience, the church office manager, walks into the kitchen and sits down beside him.

"What's on the agenda today, April?"

"You have five house visits and soup kitchen duty at one o'clock," she replies. "And don't forget confession tonight."

Visiting the sick and administering the sacraments is one of his daily obligations. He and Monsignor Bryan alternate performing house visits and hospital visits on a day-to-day basis.

"Will I need my car or am I within walking distance to all of today's visits?" he asks.

She hands him the Google map she printed out earlier and replies, "I think you'll be fine walking, unless the weather turns nasty later today."

Mrs. Sardy, a self-appointed meteorologist, glances up from her newspaper and says, "Perfect walking weather today, Father. No snow and an average temperature of fifty degrees."

"Sounds wonderful to me. One more coffee and I'll be on my way," he says, looking at Mrs. Sardy. "Anything else new in the neighborhood?"

She points at her newspaper and says, "Another drunk found beaten to death, two injured in a knife fight, an abandoned child discovered in an alley and the body of a homeless man was found dead, from the elements. Would you like me to continue?"

"No, I get the idea. Someday I'm going to ask you that question and you're going to give me some good news for a change."

"Don't hold your breath, Father," she replies sarcastically while sipping on her coffee.

"Well, I'm off. I shall see everyone later."

"Don't be late for dinner. Five-thirty sharp, Father. You, me, and pot roast."

"Ah, something to look forward to," he says with a happy chuckle.

"Be careful out there, Father."

As he walks through the dingy neighborhood, he tries to imagine what it must have been like before most of the local businesses closed and every other house with boarded windows didn't sit empty. Some of the old timers tell stories of the safe, family-friendly neighborhood that once existed in this location, but it's hard to believe it ever existed at all. They say that the streets and homes were clean, and children played on the sidewalks. There were no drive-by shootings, no drug peddlers or prostitutes on each corner, and very little crime in the area.

It's like waking up to a bad dream, thinks Father Marco, *but at least God has given us this beautiful, sunny day.*

By twelve-thirty Father Marco has completed his house visits and is on his way to help out at the soup kitchen. The soup kitchen is located in the basement of St. Anne's and manages to feed fifty to sixty poor and homeless people daily. It doesn't provide much more than soup and bread, but it's better than nothing.

During lunch, Father lectures about God's love for his children and about the power of prayer, but for the most part his words fall on deaf ears. It took a long time for him to accept the fact that no one was listening, and in the early days he would shush and chastise people who failed to pay attention. Now he doesn't really give a damn. Those who want to be saved will listen and the rest – well, he can't save them all.

After his lecture he mingles with the crowd, listens attentively to their problems, and often invites them to participate in morning mass or the Wednesday evening sacrament of confession.

Generally, he loses more souls than he saves, but every soul saved is worth the effort... or so he tells himself.

He arrives back at the rectory just in time to wash up before dinner is served. Mrs. Sardy has prepared a delicious pot roast with herb roasted potatoes and cinnamon glazed carrots. For dessert, a fresh apple pie a la mode, accompanied by a fresh pot of hot coffee. As usual, Father Marco eats too much too quickly and blames Mrs. Sardy for his ever-expanding waistline.

She laughs and replies, "Whatever happened to eating in moderation?"

"No wonder Monsignor Bryan has stuck around for twenty-five years. He's addicted to your food."

"I'll take that as a compliment, Father."

They banter back and forth as Mrs. Sardy clears the table and washes the dishes. At six-thirty her day is complete, and she bids Father Marco a restful good night.

He relishes the half hour of peace and quiet before heading to church to administer confession to the ungrateful. Closing his eyes, he dreams about his Nonna kneeling in a pew, praying for his soul. As he kneels beside her, she turns and slaps him across the face.

Shocked, he asks, "Nonna, what did I do to deserve that?"

"Don't treat me like a fool, Marco. You know exactly what you've done."

"I've done all I can to make you proud of me."

"You've lost your way, Marco, and you don't even see it. How will you save the souls of others when you can't even save your own?"

"I don't understand," he replies as the sound of a crashing cup brings him back to reality. He curses under his breath and sweeps the sharp pieces of glass into the dustpan. This isn't the first time he's had this dream, but he's still struggling to understand what it all means.

He grabs his coat and walks across the parking lot into St. Anne's. He spots Johnny praying in the front pew and notices a handful of parishioners waiting for confession. He uses the term 'parishioners' loosely because some are only here for the sacrament of confession; they never attend any other church services.

At seven o'clock Father Marco begins to receive confessions. The first confessor enters the confessional and Father can smell the alcohol on his breath.

"Bless me, Fadder, for I have sinned."

Father Marco interrupts him and asks, "Have you been drinking, son?"

"Yes, Fadder, but I know what I'm doing, and I need God to forgive me for my sins."

"And how have you sinned?"

"Last night I beat up a man and stole his money."

"Why did you do that?" Father asks, already knowing the answer.

"I needed a drink so bad" – the man hiccups – "but I didn't have no money, Fadder. I asked him to lend me some, but he said no... so I took it."

"You understand that what you did is wrong and you're sorry for what you've done," Father said.

"Yes, Fadder." The man hiccups again.

"Do you promise not to do this again?"

No response.

"Did you hear what I asked you?"

"Yes, Fadder, but I can't promise I won't do it again. When things get real bad, I do what I have to do to get what I need."

Father Marco lets out a deep breath and says, "Son, it doesn't sound to me like you're sorry for your sins, so why should God forgive you?"

"Because it's God's fault that I am the way I am. My old man was a drunk and so was my grandpa and God made us all in his likeness."

"You're very confused, son, and I can see that you need help. Do you know how to get to the corner of Broadway and First Street?"

"Sure, Fadder."

"Alcoholics Anonymous meets there every Thursday at seven o'clock. You need to be there every Thursday, and then come back when you're sober and perhaps God will forgive you for your sins. Now please leave or I will call the police and have you removed."

The drunk leaves, but not before shouting several obscenities in Father's direction and swearing never to return.

Under his breath, Father Marco says, "Good riddance, son. Remember that God helps those who help themselves."

The next confessor is another lowlife, a man named Lenny. Lenny is a pimp who wants forgiveness for beating up one of his girls, who he claims is holding out on him.

"Lenny, when are you going to stop doing Satan's work?"

"Come on, Father, cut the sermon. I'm here to be forgiven, not to listen to your holier-than-thou crap."

"Prostitution is illegal and immoral, and yet you see nothing wrong with what you're doing. You are an incredible disappointment in the Lord's eyes and yet you feel no remorse."

"Oh, dear God, where the hell is Monsignor Bryan when you need him?" Lenny says as he walks out of the confessional. "You're such a self-righteous asshole."

"Another satisfied customer," Father says to himself as he makes the sign of the cross and laughs. If this continues, he might end up strangling someone before the night is through.

The next confessor he recognizes as little Johnny Bello. Johnny comes to confess his sins once a week, even though the boy has nothing substantial to confess.

"Bless me, Father, for I have sinned. It's been one week since my last confession." Johnny pauses, then continues, "I used the Lord's name in vain twice and I raised my voice at my mother when she asked me to go to bed early last night."

Father Marco smiles and asks, "Are you sorry for your sins?"

"Yes, Father."

"Say three Our Fathers and two Hail Marys and God will forgive you. In the name of the Father, the Son, and the Holy Spirit. Amen. Go in peace, my son."

If only all confessions were as pure and heartfelt as Johnny's, then the world would be a better place.

The next four confessions are from a mishmash of neighborhood losers, all wanting forgiveness, but none truly sorry for their sins. Father Marco is developing a whopping headache and hoping there aren't too many more fakers he will need to deal with tonight.

A young woman enters the confessional and sits quietly until Father clears his throat and asks, "Can I help you, my child?"

"I don't think you can, Father," she says as she bursts into tears.

"You are in the house of God, my dear, and I'm certain that whatever you have to tell me, He will forgive you."

"I'm scared, Father. What I've done is so awful that I'm afraid God will not find it in his heart to forgive me, and I need His forgiveness."

He sits speechless listening to her sob. *What could this sweet young girl have done to feel such remorse?* he wonders.

"Tell me what is bothering you, my child, and I will help you find forgiveness."

"I don't know if I can say it, because once I tell you, then I'll know that it's real and there is no turning back."

Oh, for Pete's sake, he thinks. *Just say it and be done with all the drama,* but what comes out of his mouth is, "Take your time, dear, and let me know when you are ready to speak. There is no need to rush in the house of the Lord."

She begins to wipe her eyes as the tears slowly subside.

"Father, I k-k-killed a man and I can't get the vision of his face out of my mind."

"How did this happen?" he asks in shock.

"I was walking home from work last week when a man grabbed me and dragged me into an alley. He started to touch me all over and told me he was going to do terrible things to me. He pinned me to the ground and started tearing at my clothes. I could tell he was drunk because his breath stunk of alcohol. I begged him to stop, but he just laughed, told me to be still and I might enjoy what he had in store for me."

"As I lay on the ground, helpless, my hand brushed against an empty wine bottle, which I smashed over his head. He fell over unconscious and that's when I should have run away, but I didn't."

She begins crying again and buries her face in her hands. Father Marco is mesmerized by her story and encourages her to continue.

"I'm going to hell, Father. I just know that I'm going to hell."

"For what, my child?" he asks, bewildered. "Was it not self-defense?"

"If I had walked away and called the police, I wouldn't be feeling this way now, but Satan had other plans for me."

"Satan?" he says. "What does Satan have to do with this?"

"He made me do it, Father," she says with a frightened look on her face. "He possessed my body and made me stab the man fifty times with the sharp edges of the broken bottle."

He watches her in the glow of the confessional and thinks, *This poor girl is about to throw up or perhaps pass out.*

She regains her composure and continues her story.

"There was blood everywhere. I did all I could to keep my wits about me, but eventually I panicked, ran home and locked myself away. I've been there for the past week."

"You didn't call the police?"

"No, Father."

To her obvious surprise, Father Marco says, "You did the right thing, my child."

"What?" she says with a confused look.

"My dear, the bastard had it coming."

She bursts out laughing and says, "Easy for you to say, sitting in that seat, basking in your self-righteous purity, but I'm the one who's come within inches of committing suicide several times this week. I'm the one who can't forgive herself and is hoping that you can help me find peace with what I've done."

"My dear, I'm sure that under the circumstances, God will forgive you for your indiscretion."

"Indiscretion? Oh, that's precious, coming from someone who's never done an evil thing in his life. I guess it's easy to tell me I'm forgiven when you've never committed the atrocity I've committed. God, this was a mistake coming here."

Father Marco is beginning to dislike this young lady's attitude. Who is she to judge him? If only she knew the things he's had to endure and the acts of violence he's had to perform in God's name.

"Don't be so quick to judge me," he says defiantly. "You have no idea what you are talking about, my dear."

"Oh, come on, are you going to sit there and tell me that you've ever had to kill a man? I didn't think that priests were allowed to lie, even if they're trying to make someone feel better."

Something inside of Father Marco snaps, and he hears himself say, "My dear, you have no idea how many people I've killed in God's name."

"This is ridiculous. Of all the priests I could have come to, I had to find one who's a damn liar. I'm leaving," she says as she rises from her knees.

"Get back on your knees," he snaps a bit louder than he meant to. "I'm not finished speaking."

Shaken by his words, she drops to her knees. Judging by her expression, she can see his face glowing in anger. He then begins to tell her his frightening tales about all the men and women he has killed. The prostitute who threatened to scream rape, the drug pusher who sold to the neighborhood children, the gay transvestite who propositioned him for sex, the drunk who held a knife to his throat, the list goes on and on. By the time he stops, he's told her about twenty people that he's disposed of around the neighborhood.

"Well, Father, I guess I was wrong," she says with a shocked look. "Maybe you do know exactly what I'm going through."

Father Marco sits calmly and for the first time in years he feels at peace. He has wanted to confess his sins for so many years but was afraid that Monsignor Bryan wouldn't understand.

"Thank you, Father. You have no idea how much this means to me."

"You're welcome, my child. Now, for your penance, say ten Our Fathers and twenty Hail Marys and God will forgive you of your sin, as He has forgiven me."

"God bless you, Father."

She gets up and exits the confessional. Father Marco waits for the next confessor, but no one comes into the confessional. After waiting ten more minutes, Father looks at his watch. It's 7:55, and he decides that must be it for the night.

He makes the sign of the cross, steps out of the confessional and is surprised to find Monsignor Bryan standing in front of him.

"Monsignor, what are you doing here?" he asks in shock.

Before Monsignor Bryan can open his mouth, Father Marco's arms are pulled behind his back and he can feel cold metal snapping around his wrists. He turns and faces the young woman from the confessional, who's staring at him with a big smile on her face.

"What is the meaning of this?" he asks, outraged.

"Father Marco Mancini, you are under arrest for multiple murders. You have the right to remain silent..."

Father Marco blanks out and a vision of his Nonna appears before him, praying her rosary with tears in her eyes.

The young woman shakes him and asks, "Do you understand the rights I've just read to you?"

"Yes," he replies as his chin drops to his chest.

He hears the voice of Monsignor Bryan say, "When Detective Burrows came to me with these allegations, I told her she was crazy. I told her I knew Father Marco, and he was incapable of the acts she was accusing him of committing."

"How could you do this, Monsignor? You allowed them to set me up."

"How could you do this to *me*?" screams Monsignor Bryan. "You've made a fool of me and a mockery of the church. You and the other self-righteous people like you who have done irreparable damage to the priesthood and have diminished all the good we do in our communities and around the world."

Detective Burrows steps in and says, "Don't beat yourself up, Monsignor. It's just one man, one priest, who screwed up by taking the law into his own hands. I'm sure that people will see this for what it is and not place blame on all priests or on the church."

"I hope you're right, Detective, but right now there's a little boy behind me whose world has been shaken. What do I tell him?"

Johnny Bello stands in the first pew, a look of total horror on his face. Father Marco can hear him sniffling and see the tears on the boy's cheeks. He has no remorse for the things he's done, but the face of this little boy will haunt him for the rest of his life if he doesn't say something now.

"I need to speak to Johnny," says Father Marco.

"I don't think that's a good idea," replies Detective Burrows. "Haven't you done enough damage?"

"I need to make this right. Please let me speak to him for one moment."

After a moment of thought, Monsignor Bryan nods and asks Johnny to come to him. Johnny walks reluctantly towards them, keeping his eyes on the floor and away from Father Marco.

Father Marco kneels down on one knee in front of the boy and says, "Johnny, please look at me. There is something I want to tell you and I need you to look at me when I say it."

Johnny raises his tearful eyes and Father Marco is struck through the heart by what he sees. Trying hard to maintain his composure, he tells the boy what he needs to hear.

"Johnny, you once told me you wanted to be like me. Don't be like me. Be better than me. I know in my heart that someday you'll become a wonderful priest."

"Yes, Father Marco."

"What do you want to be when you grow up?"

"A saint," replies Johnny. "I want to be a Saint in God's army."

"How do you become a saint?"

"By joining the priesthood, spreading God's word, helping the less fortunate and defending my beliefs, no matter what."

Father Marco winks at Johnny and says, "*Bravo, caro mio. You're going to make me very proud someday.*"

A Message from the Author

I hope you enjoyed reading this book as much as I enjoyed writing it.

As a self-published independent author, I don't have the financial resources to advertise my books to a mass audience, so I rely on wonderful readers like you to help spread the word. If you enjoyed what you read, I hope you'll tell your friends and family about it.

Reviews are essential to any book's success. If you can spare a moment to leave a short review on Amazon or Goodreads it would be gratefully appreciated.

Peace.

About the Author

John D. Ottini was born in Northern Italy, raised, and educated in Canada, and currently resides in Central, Florida with his wife and a mischievous kitty named Bella.

Writing Style

Famed director Alfred Hitchcock once said, "Drama is life with the dull parts left out." That's Mr. Ottini's approach to writing a short story or novel; more meat, less filler.

He has always disliked books that doddle on and on with long descriptive passages having little to do with moving the story forward. You won't find that in his books. His writing is more in tune with the late, great, detective/mystery novelist Robert Parker's style of writing, where the story is told through fast and witty dialog.

Another aspect of the Author's writing is to incorporate twists and turns along the way, to keep the reader guessing until the end of the story. If you figure out, who did it, before the end of the story or novel, then he hasn't done his job.

If these are the type of mystery, suspense, or thriller stories you find pleasure in reading, then you will enjoy reading Mr. Ottini's books.

Social Media

Author's Blog

jdonovels.wordpress.com

Amazon Author Central Page

amazon.com/author/johnottini

Facebook

facebook.com/JohnOttiniNovels

GoodReads

goodreads.com/John_D_Ottini